FURY & VIRTUE

ALSO BY T. G. AYER

Young Adult Paranormal

THE VALKYRIE SERIES

Dead Radiance
Dead Radiance Audio
Dead Embers
Dead Embers Audio
Dead Chaos
Dead Chaos Audio
Dead Wrath
Dead Silence
Joshua - Dead Radiance
Joshua II - Dead Embers
Joshua III - Dead Chaos
Joshua IV - Dead Wrath
Joshua V - Dead Silence

THE HAND OF KALI SERIES

Fire & Shadow
Blood & Gold
Time & Fate
Fury & Virtue
Spirit & Soul

FURY & VIRTUE

T.G. AYER

AUTHORS NOTE

AUTHORS NOTE

Hindu Mythology is a living religion.
Like, Christianity, Islam, Judaism & Buddhism, Hinduism has millions of followers around the world. Fiction featuring Hindu gods is not merely a matter of choosing a god, and placing them in a fictional situation, mainly because you risk offending that deities devout worshippers. Unlike the Greek, Roman, Egyptian & Norse Pantheon, Hindu & Buddhist gods must be treated with the utmost respect in any fiction. I hope I have maintained this ethic within my series.
I have tried to maintain as much respect as possible while still using fiction to both entertain and educate the reader. The Kali series is filled with details of the various deities currently worshipped across the world.
Some rituals and powers are fiction, of course.

There is much in the Kali series that is part of my own journey in life. I hope my travels in India have lent some level of authenticity to the Indian scenes.

My familiarity with Bharathanaytam through my mother and daughter, has inspired the choice of theme for this book. I hope I've given you, the reader, some insight into the beauty of the dance style. Both Bharatnatyam and the North Indian dance style of Kathak are widely practiced so if you are interested in taking up the art, you should be able to find a teacher/school near you.

My descriptions and details regarding trance states are from having witnessed it myself. Information is available online for further reading.urney with me.

Demons, Zombies, Undead & other creatures and spirits are as per mythology texts and are available online to research. Much of how to eliminate these creatures is anecdotal & fictional. Sorry guys, if you come across a Vitala, you're on your own.

CHAPTER 1

Meeting the parents is always stressful. The only thing worse is when one parent is a god and the other a dying mortal.

Probably a good thing Maya had already met Nik's father, Yama, the God of the Underworld. Probably a good thing too, that only a few weeks ago, her actions had helped free the god of death from his captor, the demon lord Narakasura, and helped restore sanity to a world filled with the living dead.

Now, Maya tightened her fingers into a fist. Her emotions were a maelstrom of fear, doubt and nerves, but Maya tried not to let it get the best of her.

"Ready?" asked Nik softly from the sofa beside her.

Nikhil. Demigod. Son of Yama.

Maya's boyfriend.

The guy was Bollywood gorgeous, all dark shoulder-length hair, chiseled features and the blackest eyes she'd ever seen.

There was something else about him, some kind of energy he exuded, that made Maya acutely aware of his presence. Probably because she was crazy about him.

Or maybe it was his godly DNA.

Maya let out a puff of breath, the exhalation doing nothing for the conflagration in her stomach. She released the cream silk cushion she'd been suffocating to death, and gave him a tight smile. "Ready as I'll ever be."

The TV was on in the Rao's living room, but Maya barely paid attention to the Supernatural rerun. Sam & Dean had always been enough to keep her attention. Proof she wasn't as calm as she'd hoped to be.

Nick frowned. He curled a hand around her waist and leaned closer. "If you don't want to go I can cancel."

Disappointment tinged Nik's dark eyes and Maya shook her head. She put the pillow back in place, plumping it up to keep her hands busy. She'd agreed to meet his mother, and she wasn't going to break their plans now. Besides, she wanted to meet the woman who'd raised Nik, understand how she'd managed a life as the spouse of a god.

Not to mention Archana Maistry was dying. Maya wanted to get to know his mother before she died.

Because, for all intents and purposes, Maya was in a similar situation. Sure, Nik was only half a god, and sure they weren't married, but anything Nik's mom could tell her would help. She was really the only person who could speak from the experience of being in a relationship with a god.

Maya looked up at Nik. "Don't be silly. I'm just nervous. I've no intention of canceling."

"I know. But you don't have to-"

"Nik," Maya said with a low laugh. "It's normal to be nervous when meeting the parents."

Nik's forehead wrinkled and he shook his head. "I wasn't when I met your parents." Then his lips twisted as he hid a grin.

Maya punched him lightly on his shoulder and got to her feet. "Of course, you weren't. You met them before you even met me."

And it wasn't as if he'd met them as a prospective suitor for their daughter's hand. Nik had been in communication with Dev and Leela Rao as part of his responsibility as Lord Yama's right hand. He'd been tasked with the responsibility of keeping an eye on the Hand of Kali.

The Hand of Kali, aka Maya Rao.

Maya cleared her throat, then smoothed down her skirt. She'd chosen an ankle-length full-circle pink skirt, a color her mom would describe as cerise. Woven with golden thread with a paisley self-print, the skirt was subtle and still elegant with its voluminous skirt. She paired it with a soft cap-sleeved blouse, pink crystal hoop earrings, and a pair of stunning pink high-heeled sandals.

What happened to black leather and jeans, Maya wondered as she surveyed her feminine attire.

She'd been totally nervous while dressing, knowing her first impression would set the stage to the visit and not wanting to be a disappointment. She'd gone through a dozen different outfits, wishing her best friend Joss had been around to help her choose. Too bad Joss had to visit with her parents.

Straightening her spine, Maya took Nik's arm and gave him a firm nod. Her stomach lurched as they moved through dimensions and solidified inside a spacious, high-ceilinged hotel room.

Nik gave her arm a brief squeeze before he let go and walked towards a set of inner doors. The place was luxurious with airy gauze nets on the windows, framed by heavy ivory brocade drapes, with the afternoon sun searing a warm path along the cream deep pile carpets.

The decor too was elegant and feminine, lots of white fabric with subtle gold accents. She was standing in a living room, off which at least half a dozen doors led. Probably bedrooms and bathrooms, Maya assumed.

Not your standard hotel room.

Seconds later the door opened and Nik exited, accompanied by a couple. Maya was unable to hide her double-take as she took in Lord Yama, standing beside his human wife. Nik's mom was almost as tall as his dad. Her waist-length hair was midnight black, and her large green eyes glittered as she smiled at Maya.

She exuded a resonance so filled with power she could have passed for a goddess had Maya not already known she was a mere mortal. Her aquamarine maxi dress and spaghetti straps would make the case for mortal, but Maya had to wonder.

She didn't miss the older woman's amused expression at her reaction to the handsome god in modern clothing. Lord Yama wore a pair of dark jeans, a long sleeved Henley shirt and black sneakers. You could pass him on the street and have no clue as to the power he possessed.

Yama smiled and nodded at Maya. "Thank you for coming, Maya."

Maya hesitated, her heart slamming against her ribs as if wanting out. Had she been summoned without her knowledge? Despite her confusion, she smiled and said, "I wouldn't miss it."

He nodded approvingly, then held a hand out to Maya, beckoning her closer. Nik stood at his mother's side, oddly silent.

Maya stepped closer and Lord Yama drew his wife to him. He smiled from her to Maya, then met his wife's eyes. "This is Maya Rao." Maya noticed he didn't get too formal and neither did he mention the word 'girlfriend'. She wasn't sure what that meant, but she smiled as the god continued, "And Maya, this is Archana, Nik's mother."

Maya reached out and took Archana's hand, surprised Nik's mom looked younger than her eighty-something years. In fact, she looked about Yama's age, early fifties maybe, though God knows how old *he* was.

Maya swallowed down her nerves. "It's lovely to meet you." As she spoke, Maya's cheeks grew hot. She had no idea how to address the woman. Nik's mother deserved a more respectful salutation than just her first name.

What nerves Maya had disappeared as Archana reached for her and drew her into a warm hug. When she released Maya, she said, "I'm so glad to finally meet you Maya. Nikhil has told me so much about you."

Heat bloomed in Maya's cheeks and she glanced at Nik who stood just behind his mom. What had he told his mother? But she didn't have time to think about it as Archana drew her to the sitting area and pulled her down beside her.

"Now, I want to hear everything. Nikhil told me you had a bit of an adventure a few weeks back. I admit he did give me the Cliff's Notes version, but I wanted the hot details direct from the source."

Maya grinned and relaxed at last. "It's not all that exciting, to be honest."

Archana raised a dark eyebrow. "*I* shall be the judge of that. Now spill."

CHAPTER 2

The only moment Nik and Maya had to themselves was when he returned her to her house after midnight, the silence of the house duplicitous. Either sleep or work would provide such a dead calm.

Nik had barely taken a breath before Maya rounded on him, keeping her voice low in deference to sleeping occupants. "I thought you said your mom was old?"

Nik chuckled as Maya drew him into the kitchen. "Yeah. About that . . ."

The kitchen held a hint of her mom's special Tikka Masala chicken and though Maya wasn't exactly starving, she didn't miss a step as she grabbed plates and glasses, and warmed a few pieces of the delicious meal.

As she worked, she glanced over her shoulder at Nik who was attending to their drinks. "So?"

Nik cleared his throat and paused just as he was about to pour cranberry juice into their glasses. "My father finally managed to convince her to take the Amrita."

Maya's movements stilled. The Amrita was the elixir of Life.

The goddess Varuni herself created the elixir and Maya knew first-hand how precious the drink was.

The gods used the elixir from time to time to sustain them during their extended lives, and in the past Yama's human wife had refused to take it, preferring her mortality to living an immortal life just because of her relationship with a god.

"Holy wow. That must have been a relief for the two of you?" She forced herself to move, bringing the warmed chicken and a bowl of fragrant yellow rice to the table.

Nik nodded as he finished pouring, then sat on his stool. "We were more than relieved."

"What made her change her mind?"

Nik looked up at Maya and grinned. "Maybe it's because I told her about *you?*"

She frowned. "What do I have to do with it?"

He shrugged. "Nothing directly. She said she realized then there was a future to be had and if she chose to die then she was choosing to miss out on my future as well as my father's."

"That's both very sad and very sweet." Maya sighed.

Nik smiled and reached for the chicken. He served them both as Maya did the same with the rice.

How very domestic.

Nik had healed fairly quickly after being stabbed in the neck by the demon lord Kas. Plus, he'd fidgeted around the last few days, making Maya more certain he was itching to return to doing something with his time other than watching movies and visiting historical sites around the world.

They'd made a few pit-stops, the Colosseum, Machhu Picchu, the Great Wall of China. But one can only do so much traveling before it becomes tiresome. Maya had split her time between Nik and her mother who were both recovering from the poison with which Kas had laced his daggers.

And school.

Thank goodness her parents had had the foresight to begin

homeschooling. It gave Maya and Joss the flexibility to train, handle cases, and recuperate where necessary.

Leela had also made steady progress, purging the poison from her system with the help of the power of the goddess Bhumi.

Maya still found it hard to believe her own mother was the avatar of the Goddess of the Earth. But then, it made perfect sense for Kali to send Maya to Leela to raise. Even that convoluted reasoning was beginning to make sense to Maya, which should definitely be something to worry about.

After nibbling a drumstick, Maya asked, "So when do you get back to normal work?" Maya understood now that Archana's decision must also have had something to do with his time off.

He wiped his mouth with a paper napkin, and took a sip of his juice. Then he cleared his throat and said, "Today if I wanted. My father asked if I was ready."

Maya nodded.

It was time for him to return to work.

She pursed her lips. "Unfortunately, all vacations must come to an end."

Nik laughed. "It's been fun while it lasted.

Nik left soon after, with a promise to update her on when he would return to work proper, and Maya trudged up to bed enveloped by the hollow sound of darkness and night. For some reason, the nighttime seemed to promise ghosts and ghouls and not the usual peace and regeneration.

Not surprising with the life Maya led.

Her dad's study was empty, and she suspected he was out on a case. She tiptoed upstairs, ensuring the sound of her heels on the wood floor wouldn't wake anyone up. Her parent's room lay submerged in darkness, with her mom's form unmoving on the bed beneath a burgundy and gold silk comforter, a get-well present to Leela from the goddess Chayya.

The goddess of shadows had dropped by every so often to check on the family, but Maya hadn't seen much of her in the last week or so. Guess even gods got too busy to waste time on friends.

Sabala, Maya's personal bodyguard in the form of an honest-to-goodness hound from hell, gifted to her by Lord Yama, sat at the foot of her mom's bed, watching over her.

Leela had spent days sleeping during her recovery, but in the last two weeks she'd been up and about, frustrated she couldn't get back to work.

Maya totally understood where she was coming from, and had sympathized. But in the end her mom was truly better, pronounced free of the poison just last week by the goddess Chayya.

Maya headed to her bedroom after checking if Joss was home. Joss was fast asleep too, a soft snore reverberating across the room.

Her best friend, Joss Cawood, was back from a short visit with her parents who'd returned home for a brief respite from their international jet-setting lifestyle. With Joss's father playing the stock market and her mother a die-hard socialite, the couple barely had time for Joss who they'd long considered a very independent child. For years, Maya's parents had given Joss a home away from her own.

Satisfied, Maya walked to her room, by now used to the absence of the hellhound. With Nik around so often she hadn't needed the dog's protection, so he'd been charged with her mom's protection. A perfect companion dog.

Changing into her pajamas, Maya fell into bed, and stared at the ceiling where she saw Archana's face hovering above her. She'd been welcoming and pleasant and so kind. More than Maya had ever expected, especially considering how aloof Lord Yama had been in the time she'd known him.

Funny the man she'd met only a few hours ago seemed so different from the god she'd met months ago.

Maya drifted off to sleep, her thoughts filled with images of the gods she'd met, gods who'd helped her find a new place for herself in this world.

CHAPTER 3

The steady beat of the drums echoed around her, reverberating from the soft soles of her bare feet and through her bones, as if the very ground beneath her thundered with the heartbeat of Bhumi, the earth mother.

Her feet hit the ground, flat of the foot first, hard enough to slap the cracked stone with a sharp tap, then up on the ball, knee bent, stance elegant, channeling musical energy from the air around her. The thick and well-worn leather belt at her ankles, threaded with hundreds of tiny brass bells, jingled, tinkling in accompaniment to the rhythm of the drums.

She was ready, her pose expectant as the drumbeats teased her chakras, her hip jutting out almost provocatively, her hands folded demurely over her right hip bone. She lifted her chin, dark kohl-lined eyes gazing upward, a hint of an entranced smile cast up at an unseen but benevolent moon -- the god Chandra smiling down upon his devotee.

The dance, each movement, each sequence, telling a tale so familiar, so tangible.

Around her, the temple hall lay empty, stone walls smoothed after hours of laboring now cracked by the snaking roots and vines. Delicate alcoves once populated by an abundance of hand-carved stone statues of the gods, now bathed in layers of dust and covered with a dense, sickly green moss.

The vine-covered walls of the temple rose high above, disappearing into a darkness filled with the hanging roots of thick plant growth. Somewhere high above her something scurried, a creature seeking a hiding place, or waiting to pounce.

But she was not afraid.

In this mostly-abandoned temple, high up in the mountains of Southern India, giant statues dotted the floor space, standing twenty feet in height and serving as columns to support a once-majestic roof.

The temple was seldom used by the villagers, and populated mostly by reclusive priests who flitted its halls like ghostly apparitions.

Too large to be looted, the statues remained, now overrun by vines and moss. Despite the overgrowth, the carvings, never painted, never adorned by color, remained infinitely beautiful in their simplicity.

Only the flickering light from dozens and dozens of clay lamps held the darkness at bay, the odor of hot oil and flame drifting lazily toward her, teasing her nostrils. The lamps cast ghostly shadows across the uneven walls. Shadows that danced and shivered, waiting for her to join them.

Again the drums beat, throbbing in time with the pulsating of her heart. Dressed in a simple red sari, pleated loosely around the legs to allow for movement, shot with gold thread to capture the glow of the lamplight, the girl stood as still as the carved gods, glittering in the shimmering lights, waiting for the note that would bid her begin.

Another beat.

She extended her foot, and drew her toes across the floor in a wide semicircle. The silver rings on her toes glinted as she stepped to the side, planting her foot on the ground before transferring her weight to it. The bells sang again, their music a multitude of sweet notes of pure sound.

The beat of the drum wove an intoxicating spell around her, and she found herself drifting away to that place she always visited at the height of the dance, a place of utter peace and tranquility. Where, while she danced, while her body moved in time with music that swelled around her, she remained in total harmony with the universe.

The drumbeat sped up, and her heart kept time, escalating with anticipation. She lifted her intricately hennaed hands, palms placed together in holy salutation, raising them to the East where Surya rose from the darkness, to bless the land with his benevolent light.

From somewhere beyond the drums came the undulating song of a flute, drifting on the air, the notes clear and beautiful, the sound of sunshine on ice, of the ocean at its depths.

Her body swayed, sinuous and entrancing in time with the notes, slow, dreamy movements that picked up pace along with the music. The music echoed around her, earnest and sad and yet still as intoxicating as the beat of the drum.

The temple was her solace. She came here to practice, to be surrounded by the benevolence of her god. The eternal Lord of the Universe, the cosmic dancer Lord Nataraja.

Before her, in the largest alcove, stood a stone carving of her Lord. He rose into the air, almost touching the stone ceiling. Even now as she stood waiting for that one special beat that would bid her begin, she adored the statue with her gaze. She'd spent hours staring at the sculpture, marveling at the workmanship; what talent the sculptor had had to hammer stone flames that looked real enough to singe one's skin.

The statue gleamed, free of cracks and overgrowth, as if naturally repelling the onslaught of the jungle. The Lord in defiance of the nature he kept in perpetual balance.

The music quickened, and her heart followed suit, slamming

against her ribs in anticipation. She began to dance, slapping a foot on the stone, once, twice. Then again, keeping the beat. Creating with her feet, her own music.

She moved faster now, stamping each foot on the stone floor in time to the beat of the drum, a rhythmic pattern, faster and faster as she moved.

Her swaying hands lifted, formed shapes as she nodded and smiled, speaking a silent language, as she told a story with her eyes and her body, as she performed her prayer to her lord. She had to remind herself to breathe, remind herself to remain in control. It was so easy for the music and the dance to take over, so easy to be swept away by the joy of it all.

When she'd first learned the art of Bharatanatyam, she'd heard of the trance. It was said to be the ultimate level of dance, usually only attained by a Kumari after years, sometimes even decades.

Up here in the mountains, the simple folk rarely had the privilege of educated dance teachers. Here they made do, learning from the older women, and passing the art down one generation at a time.

But even here, the legend of the trance was repeated in hushed whispers. Some said the dancer communed with Lord Nataraja when deep within their trance, a blessing dreamed of by many, and experienced by precious few.

For that reason, she'd never revealed her first experience to her mother. She'd been dancing a mere two years now, since her fourteenth birthday, and already for the past year she had experienced the joy of the trance.

She feared the danger of it only because she had no control. When she fell into the grip of the trance she knew nothing until she opened her eyes again, and often she'd find herself lying on the floor exhausted, hours later.

Despite the danger, she'd risk it time and time again, just for the beauty of the trance, risk too, the possibility of discovery. The meager contingent of priests knew she danced here, and they accommodated her, smiling benevolently whenever she arrived.

But they were not the only ones to use the temple. She had to stop being careless.

For now, she slipped deeper into the joy, and allowed herself the freedom.

To dance, faster and faster, the energy taking control of her body and of her mind. She gasped for breath as dizziness rose like a tide, eager to overcome her. Heat filled her body, flooding her veins, burning her blood.

The music echoed in her ears, a distant sound drifting to her from beyond her awareness. And still she danced, swirling around the room, as perspiration tickled, drifting down her spine, as the cool air of the South Indian night whispered against her slick skin.

And then a light flickered. At the end of her vision, the softest glow.

She blinked. Had she imagined the golden light? Had it been a trick of flames, a reflection perhaps.

Her chest tightened as trepidation stabbed her heart.

She wanted to stop dancing, to search the growing darkness enveloping her, but her body no longer obeyed.

Still she wasn't truly afraid.

She continued to dance, though a part of her brain tried to remain aware. And when she blinked again, golden light shimmered just beyond her sight, growing ever brighter around her. The flames of hundreds of clay lamps danced upon the walls, filling the room with fiery light.

As she moved, she spun on her heel, sinking into a bow, scanning the temple hall. The pale grey stone, now awash with gold, glittered.

The light beckoned her filling her spirit, teasing her consciousness, threatening to toss her into the waiting darkness.

Her muscles ached now, her feet throbbing, but her heart

swelled, filled with inexplicable passion and energy. She both loved and hated this part -- where her spirit filled with endless joy, the stage she strived to attain every single time.

Fatigue pulled at her limbs, weighing them down, and yet she didn't stop.

She was unable to stop.

She'd concluded the dance, prayed it would signal the end of her torture. But her limbs moved, her own will ignored.

Her heart raced now, edged with fear, yet still in time with the music. She strained, urging her body to stop dancing, but still she moved.

A cry of fear escaped her throat as her mind slipped back into the reality of the dance. The trance no longer held, and she was horribly aware of her bloodied feet, and her aching muscles. Her clothes stuck to her skin, soaked with sweat.

Yet she still danced, her movements frenzied, the chaos of hurricanes tearing through her heart, of mountains come crashing down when the earth rebelled.

Tears slipped from her eyes, her muscles aching, filled with intense pain, dancing even when her feet began to slip on the bloody stone floor. Fear filled her throat, thick and cloying. But still she moved with the music, her body intent on screaming its own physical song, in harmony with the drums, with sorrow.

She watched herself now, part of her awareness splitting away, watched as she danced around the temple floor leaving a trail of slick red behind her. She watched the white stone of the Nataraja begin to glow with an inner fire.

Her heart slammed against her ribs so hard it took her breath away.

Had her god come down to bless her?

But Lord Nataraja was a benevolent god. Never one to cause his devotees to suffer. She loved to dance, found utmost peace in every movement, but now every breath was filled with the fiery pain.

This was no blessing of God.

Terror cut a burning swathe through her senses.

Her black hair swung limply against her cheek, stray locks now soaked with sweat. She swayed, exhaustion urging her down, controlling her movements.

Gone was the beauty of the dance, the lithe sinuous movements. Now, she swung helplessly, a marionette controlled by insanity. Her arms flailed, whispering only the language of extreme exhaustion.

She cried out, but no sound left her throat.

Fear filled her heart.

The speed of the music increased, and the light blinded her. And she danced. It wasn't physically possible. This was a fact even a simple village girl like her knew. As exhausted as she was, to continue dancing with this much passion, and with this much pain, was simply not possible.

Darkness began to fold over her, drawing her into unconsciousness. The promise of release.

Now she prayed for the blackness.

All she had to do was give in, and she'd be free from this horror. She blinked harder, as shadows swirled within the temple. Her vision darkened further, and at last she fell to the ground, sightless, her fingers scrabbling at the curving roots.

She lay there, flat on her stomach, gasping for air, feeling the cool stone against her heated cheek. Her heart threatened to shatter her ribs, and she knew it would explode.

And she welcomed it.

One last ragged breath. A sharp stabbing speared her heart.

Fire and energy surged through her body, and she let out a slow, deep breath.

A breath that was her last.

CHAPTER 4

VOICES CALLED to Maya, hollow and echoing around her.

Scared voices.

No, terrified cries. Maya blinked, her lashes heavy as she stared blindly, confused.

She lay on the tiled floor in the front hall of her home, staring at the elegantly patterned crown molding floating where wall and ceiling met. For some reason she was beginning to think the design had been a brilliant idea.

Maya frowned, pulling her thoughts away from home decor, thinking the least someone could do was to turn the lights down before they blinded her permanently.

She blinked again, then shut her eyes, her lids heavy, too heavy to keep open.

What was she doing here, anyway?

The last thing she remembered was being in bed, and struggling to fall asleep. The cold of the marble floor bit into her skin, mean teeth relentlessly gouging to her bones.

Wait, what? Why is my skin hot?

Why am I lying on the floor?

A warm hand touched her cheek, and her mom's gentle voice drifted through the fog, the sound of comfort and safety wrapping around her like a fire-warmed blanket. "Honey, are you okay? What happened?"

Maya tried to open her eyes again, but her lids refused to obey.

She gave up.

Another voice, her dad now. "Maya, what's going on? Are you dreaming?"

Maya's forehead furrowed as memories of the dream came flooding back to her, images jostling to be the first one she recalled. She gasped and a tremor ran through her body, rippling through her limbs like an earthquake.

Movement at Maya's right drew her attention as her mom placed an arm around her, gently curling her hand around Maya's waist. She lifted Maya upright then settled her back, using the slim line of her own body to support her daughter's limp frame.

The warmth of her mom's skin gave her some comfort, fighting the incessant waves of cold that had claimed her entire body. Warmth slowly enveloped cold, battling its way through Maya's limbs, and the shivering gradually ceased.

Maya's own fire remained absent.

Awareness increased with each blink, each soft inhalation. Her breathing returned to normal. She cracked heavy lids open, and found herself surrounded by her family. Maya's dad and section chief at the KALIMA Agency, watched her from her right, meeting his wife's eyes, his own worried expression matching hers.

Sabala, sat on the floor beside the hall table which now stood at a strange angle from the wall, as if someone had bumped into it in the rush to get to Maya.

Her mom's excellent-fake Ming Dynasty vase sat on its side, having rolled almost to the edge of the table. She wanted to warn her mom, to tell her to grab the vase before it rolled over to its death, but she couldn't open her mouth.

Instead she watched Sabala as he sat watching her like a black statue, all four of his black glistening eyes staring at her as if she'd done something wrong. What did he have to be indignant about anyway?

Maya's dad slipped his arm around her waist, supporting her, giving her more of his warmth.

At Maya's feet sat her best friend Joss, the look of horror on her face visible despite her thick glasses. Joss's hair was up in rollers, hidden by an ugly yellow beanie which hurt Maya's eyes more than the light did. Despite her appearance, Joss failed to look comical, even with her expression bordering on overstated horror.

"What the hell is going on, Maya?" asked Joss, pulling her pajama shirt closed.

A distant part of Maya's mind registered the chill in the hallway, as if a North Wind had taken up residence there, and now lingered, biting at her cheeks and nipping at the tips of her ears. It was the front end of winter after all. Although a California winter wasn't something to fear, even at the worst of times.

Maya frowned.

Then why the hell is it so darned cold?

"You scared us half to death." Joss wrapped her arms around her torso, the goosebumps on her neckline confirming the low temp.

Maya turned her head slowly, relieved to see she was able to move now. The details of the dream drifted back to her.

"I was dreaming." Then she gave a cheery laugh, the sound sharp and tinny even to her ears. "More like a nightmare to be honest."

Leela squeezed her daughter a little harder. "Honey, you weren't dreaming. You were sleepwalking."

Her father laughed. His mirth sounded hollow, as if he was

pretending to be fine when all he wanted to do was give in to panic. "That was not sleepwalking. More like sleep dancing," he said.

Maya looked up at her mom. "I was dancing?" It seemed unlikely, what with Maya's sad lack of skills in anything requiring rhythm and grace.

But Leela nodded, her eyes filled with shock and amazement, in spite of the worry shadowing them. Her mom was too weak for all this drama and Maya felt a rush of guilt for forcing her out of her bed in the middle of the night. "You were dancing. For all the years you refused to learn, the way you moved just now . . . seems you have natural talent."

Maya grunted, the sound a dozen razors scraping her throat. "You and I both know I have absolutely no clue how to dance. I was born with two left feet, Mom. Even *you* have said it."

"That's what we always thought," Leela said evenly, her tone forced and edged with fear. "Only, we just saw it with our own eyes."

"You were amazing," said Joss. She too was staring at Maya in admiration.

Undeserved admiration.

Maya laughed. "It was just a dream. I must've been re-enacting what I was experiencing."

"But it doesn't make any sense." Dev got to his feet, at last doing something with himself rather than sitting still.

He was still dressed in dark jeans and a brown wooly jumper, which meant he'd come back late from whatever he'd been working on and hadn't yet gotten to bed.

Without warning, he bent and scooped Maya up in his arms, and Maya caught sight of her reflection in the gilt-edged mirror above the off-set hall table. Her face was pale, almost gray, her lips shadowed, her eyes staring as if half-crazed. No wonder these guys were concerned.

Sabala's nails scrabbled against the tiles as he got to his feet to follow them.

Dev carried her to the living room while Joss kept pace as if she thought Dev would drop Maya on her head. Her dad deposited her gently onto the sofa and sat on the arm. He put enough distance between them that she'd feel reassured as opposed to claustrophobic.

Leela followed two steps behind, and sank down beside her. Now *she* looked unsure what to do. In the end, she took Maya's icy hand, holding it gently in hers as if Maya was suddenly made of fragile porcelain.

With her whole family around her Maya was beginning to feel a little human again.

Seemed Sabala was concerned too as he came to sit in front of her, squeezing himself between the sofa and the coffee table. He lowered his head to the seat beside her knees and she smiled. The hellhound had never been super affectionate and this reaction was enough to tell her he was worried. She reached out and gave him a reassuring scratch behind the ears.

Joss sat on the very edge of the sofa opposite Maya, watching from afar as if the distance would help her not freak out.

Maya sighed, her body heavy with exhaustion. She was sinking against her mom's silk cushions, relief seconds away, when she stiffened suddenly, forcing herself to sit upright. She wrinkled her nose and shivered as her cold, sodden blue pajamas settled against her skin.

With two fingers, she pulled the front of the flannel shirt away from her skin. "Gross." She shivered lightly. "In the dream, I could see myself sweating, I could see blood on my feet."

Sabala lifted his head, then sniffed as he glanced down at Maya's feet. She leaned over and stared down in horror, studying her bleeding feet. When she glanced out into the hall, she froze. Angry red streaked the white marble, the floor not too different from those murder scenes you see on TV.

Maya lifted her feet slowly off her mom's pristine cream carpet - which was probably too late considering the splotches of red already marring its perfection -and pointed her swollen toes at her mom. Leela's expression darkened at the sight of them, and for once she didn't complain about soiling her precious carpets.

As much as Maya had endeavored to ensure her mom was fully aware that Maya was totally capable of taking care of herself, Leela still managed to coddle her daughter as if she'd remained five-years-old for more than the last decade. But, to her credit, right now she didn't go momma-bear nuts.

Instead, she released Maya's hands and got to her feet, mentioning something about wet towels. But Maya reached for her. She wasn't concerned about the wounds.

Her fire would do its job just as soon as she got the chance to concentrate. Although she'd healed herself with her fire power before - granted to her by the goddess Kali - Maya wasn't as adept at the task as she would like. And the last thing she could do was to concentrate well enough while surrounded by her family and in so much pain.

Wouldn't want any accidental redirections of fire and flame.

"What the hell is going on?" said Joss as Leela sank to the cushions, looking troubled. The hellhound whined softly, as if he too wanted to know.

"You said that already," said Maya, rolling her eyes.

"And I'll say it again."

"Please don't."

"Fine," said Joss in a huff.

Maya studied her swollen feet and sighed. Even she could see things were well past bad and clocking up to solid crazy.

"In the dream, the floor was streaked with blood. And I was dancing and dancing and I couldn't stop. And then I fainted. The last thing I remember is lying face down on the stone floor. Exactly the way I woke up." Maya looked at her dad. "How long was I dancing?" she asked softly.

Dev leaned forward, placing his elbow on his knees. He was the picture of relaxed and yet the chords in his neck stood tight. He shook his head. "Honestly? I have no idea. I was in the study and heard noises. When I came out, I saw you spinning like Fred was about to come dancing through the front door."

"Fred?" Maya frowned, her tone confused.

"Astaire." Leela's eyebrows curved dangerously.

"Who?" asked Maya, her expression deadpan.

"Maya!" Three voices protested Maya's ignorance in unison.

"Geez. I'm kidding, okay," she said, shaking her head. "I know who Fred is. Besides, wrong type of dance."

She eyed her dad, urging him to continue. He did, although he failed to stop smiling, which Maya counted as a good thing. A little distraction never hurt.

"Seemed strange," he said as he thought it over, his eyebrows scrunching. "You didn't seem to be aware of me or anything else. Kept bumping into furniture. So I called your mother."

"Why didn't you just wake me?" Maya asked, looking from one parent to the other, a little annoyed now. Her pain would certainly have been curtailed had they awakened her faster. Maya felt a rush of anger at her parents. Sabala shifted beside her knee, bumping against her either in comfort or admonition of her feelings.

Leela raised a single eyebrow this time. The woman had sharp eyes.

"Because we know from experience how dangerous pulling someone straight out of a trance can be." Leela stared at Maya, her expression dark with concern. "Waking someone while they're in the deepest part of a trance can render the person a vegetable. Not something we would treat lightly. You were dancing. It may have been a dream. But it could have been a trance. Neither of which were obvious to us at the time. Since we were smart enough not to mess with a trance, we elected to do nothing."

Elected?

When Leela used highfalutin synonyms, even Maya knew the woman was too close to being 'officially pissed off'.

Maya stiffened.

"Trance?" she said softly. "What trance? I've never had one."

Thank goodness.

Maya suppressed a shudder. She knew well enough about Trance States. The trance was a state of hyper-awareness - or non-awareness depending on who you talked to - experienced by ardent devotees, usually only at extremely religious events, and under well-supervised conditions. She'd been to mass celebrations before where hundreds of people gathered to sing, invoke trances and pierce their bodies with all manner of decorations in the name of the gods. She'd been partially fascinated and mostly horrified.

And yet, despite what her eyes had told her, despite seeing for herself needles that pierced skin without shedding a drop of blood, without leaving a single scar behind, she'd rolled her eyes at the entire act, thinking how silly it all sounded when people claimed the worshipper was channeling their god.

Not silly anymore.

Especially not when Maya had come face-to-face with a number of living deities in the past months. She'd never believed in God. Any god. She'd never thought they'd existed.

Recently she'd learned better.

"Maybe you haven't experienced a trance state in the past, but you certainly have now," said Dev. He still hadn't moved. "And nobody can rule out the possibility of experiencing one in the future."

That did not sound good.

CHAPTER 5

$\mathcal{M}$aya shivered and her Mom reached out for her. "Come, let's get you out of those clothes before you catch cold."

With a single roll of her eyes, Maya said, "Mom? How in the world would someone who has the ability to create fire catch cold?"

Leela just watched, unamused as her daughter drew her fire from her core and allowed it to rise towards her skin. There the heat collected, to be transferred to the fabric of her pajamas. And within seconds, the moisture began to rise like a mist from the wet cloth. Minutes later, the water evaporated and the fabric was dry.

And toasty warm.

I'm my very own heater.

Yay.

"There," she said, satisfied. "All done. Happy?" she asked her mom, hiding a smile as the hellhound whuffed and shifted his body away from her heated limbs.

Leela snorted and got to her feet, smoothing down the front

of her pajamas. "I'll get you something to drink. And then you can tell us more about the dream.

Before Leela hurried off, as was her way because she never did anything lazily, Maya said, "I don't want something to drink. I'd rather tell you exactly what I remember now, because I feel like the memory is drifting away." Something twisted urgently within her gut as she spoke, underlining her words.

Leela sat beside Maya, and listened as she went over the details of the dream. Even as she repeated the sequence of her memories, her heart rate sped up in response to the experience. Sabala whined softly and bumped her hand with his nose, the cool wetness of it bringing her back to awareness.

But had it truly been a trance state?

She found herself unable to accept it. Not that she didn't believe what her family had witnessed.

It just seemed too far-fetched. There must be a more accept-able reason.

When she finally finished her tale, Dev said. "It's possible this was not a dream."

Confusion clouded her brain. "If not a dream then what could it be?" she asked softly, talking more to herself than her dad.

He lifted a shoulder. "Any number of things. You could be having some sort of premonition."

Maya looked away. "There is another option."

"Which is?" asked Leela, leaning forward.

"I could just be finally going crazy. It was bound to happen."

Joss snorted and Maya's parents merely looked at each other and shook their heads.

"There is one more thing you haven't considered," said Dev, his expression far from amused.

Maya looked at him expectantly. Even Sabala shifted his glossy black eyes toward Dev.

"You could be channeling someone else. Which means we

need to find out who this person is, and if she is okay. She may be far more injured than you are right now."

Maya sighed softly and leaned back against the cushions. "There's never any peace around here, is there?"

Joss let out a tinny laugh. "Trust you to think of it that way. Anyway, I've called Nik. He'll be here any minute."

Maya glared at her. "Why did you go and do that?" Sleep-walking hardly warranted disturbing Nik, although Maya suspected he wouldn't appreciate being left out of the loop.

Now, Joss rolled her eyes dramatically. "Why do you think? You need help. Nobody here has a clue as to how to help you. No offence," she said, glancing at Maya's mom and dad.

Dev waved a hand airily. "None taken."

Maya let out a huff of breath, spine tense with irritation. Her emotions seemed all over the place. "I hope bringing him here for a stupid dream is worth it. Nik's got better things to do than assist with sleep therapy. For all we know he's returned to Florida to be with his mom."

Shaking her head, Joss said, "A little mother-son chat in the early hours of the morning?" Joss snorted. "What just happened here wasn't your run-of-the mill sleepwalking session. He'll be pissed we didn't tell him. I'm just keeping my ass out of trouble."

"It was pretty freaky," said Leela. Her gray skin and from the hollows under her eyes it was clear to Maya that she was straining herself. Trust Maya to do something to set her mom's recovery back just when she was getting back to normal. Leela smiled and patted Maya's shoulder.

"Nik will know more about the dancing in the trance thing, honey." Then Leela pointed at Maya's bloody feet. "Let's get those seen to while we wait for him."

She glanced at her mom, wondering if she meant she'd use the earth goddess's powers to try and heal Maya. She'd pull the parent card and insist, but Maya didn't plan on allowing her mom to strain herself that way. Way too soon for her to be pushing herself with healing even if she was a goddess reborn.

Maya scooted forward to step gingerly onto her feet. Her bloodied toes were about to hit the carpet when Dev heaved a deep sigh, rose to his feet and lifted her in his arms. Again.

"Good thing I'm light," she said primly as she stared up at him. "Wouldn't want you to break your back or anything."

Dev merely shook his head and headed for the stairs. Sabala snorted, got to his feet and circumnavigated Dev, as if approving of his decision to carry her. The dog followed solemnly as her dad carried Maya upstairs to her bedroom.

Things were getting a little too crazy around here.

Maya decided she'd wait to hear what Nik had to say and if she wasn't satisfied with his explanation she'd planned to do the next best thing.

Talk to a god.

CHAPTER 6

Maya's dad laid her on her bed and said, "I'll grab the first aid kit." As he left, the hellhound trotted to her bedside where again he laid his head on the mattress and stared up at her.

Guess you're back to guarding me now, right?

Sabala was always graceful, always aloof so Maya wondered what was his problem. He suddenly seemed worried, or upset she'd been hurt by her trance dance.

Maya suppressed the urge to roll her eyes again. Dev Rao's first aid kit was the size of a freaking suitcase. And besides, he won't be needing it.

She could not understand where the cuts had come from, or what exactly she'd done to break the skin open that way. Dancing meant a lot of stamping of feet against ground, but how hard would one have to stamp before skin broke anyway?

Maya brought her feet close to her body in an open yoga sit and studied the damage as the hellhound let out a soft whine. Was that the dog's way of expressing his own shock at the state of her feet?

The fleshiest parts of her soles were slashed open, blood

seeping through and drying in the gaping mouths of the wounds. Her feet still looked like a bloody mess.

Nik had taught her well, and she'd used the power to heal her body before.

She took her foot and placed it on her thigh, in a half yoga pose, giving Sabala a warning glare. She didn't need to be disturbed. Wrapping her hands around her foot, she sighed and listened to the silence around her.

Relaxing, she concentrated on her solar plexus, sinking into the simmering energy within her main chakra. Slowly she pushed the power toward her feet, forcing her legs to relax as the energy rippled along her muscles, sending sparks of heat through her flesh.

Her palms burned with fire, a simmering heat which she focused on her foot, allowing the energy to fill the muscles and tendons, to warm the broken skin and torn blood vessels.

She could feel the fire working, the energy of it seeping into her skin. She'd never understood the concept of energy being light and light being creation.

Not until Nik had taught her how to use her fire to heal.

It had been small things in the beginning; a broken fingernail, or shallow cut. Now her wounds were much bigger, much deeper, and it took her a lot longer than she expected.

Inside her feet, she could feel the fire simmer, surging through her muscles, waiting for Maya's next instruction. With a soft sigh, Maya pushed the energy through the muscles and flesh, guiding it to her dermal layer.

In the last few weeks she'd been studying anatomy, especially where it was related to her powers and how they worked. It helped that her parents, and Joss's, had transferred the two girls into the homeschool system where they could study while still training and working within the KALIMA Agency.

Maya stifled a gasp as heat pulsed through her epidermis and coiled within the broken skin of both her feet. She didn't need to look to know the damaged tissue was healing, and the broken flesh was regenerating and knitting together.

The effort to concentrate her fire on healing took a toll on her own energy, especially after what had seemed like hours of dancing. Maya felt a pull of dizziness, as if she was about to nod off to sleep. Or worse, pass out. The hellhound growled, a low rumble that made Maya blink off the blanket of fog.

Thanks, pooch.

Still, when she'd completed the first round of healing, her skin was pink and flushed with blood, and the cuts were much shallower and beginning to scab over.

Her foot, though, was still purple. And blue.

But it was looking a damn sight better than it did ten minutes ago.

Maya reached for her other foot and repeated the process. She shook her head and focused as the hellhound lifted his head of the bed and watched her intently.

A minute or so more would do the trick.

When the blast of heat dissipated, Maya shifted to the edge of the mattress and set her feet on the carpet at the side of her bed. Sabala got to his feet too, walking closer to her as if saying he'll support her.

Maya didn't decline the offer.

Placing a hand on his shoulder, she slowly placed her weight on her damaged feet and managed to rise to her feet without crying out in pain.

Holding onto Sabala she walked around the bed, then back again, wanting to be sure she'd done a good job. Her feet were throbbing by the time she returned to sit back on the edge of the bed. As she released the hellhound's silky fur, she exhaled a sigh of relief.

She'd just shifted back onto the pillows against the headboard when her parents filed into her room.

Sabala returned to the foot of the bed, head now held high in standard sentry position and Maya wondered if his emotional reaction to her injuries was out of character, or if he was just good at hiding his feelings.

Dev placed the first aid kit on the bed beside Maya, while her mother sat on the other side of her, a stack of warm wet towels on a steel tray.

Maya stared at the bag then looked up to meet her dad's eyes. "It's not necessary, Dad. The healing's done."

All he did was raise an eyebrow, then reach over to grab a towel from her Mom's tray. When Leela made a move to grab a towel Maya reached out and gripped her wrist.

"Mom. You need to rest. I'm fine. I'll wash it off in the shower."

"Maya," Leela said with a note of warning in her voice that would have made her worry if her mom wasn't so weak.

"Mom, I wouldn't lie to you. I healed the worst of it. And you know you don't have to worry about infection. I'll just send regular blasts of heat into the wound area to ward off any possible infection."

Leela hesitated then shared a concerned glance with her husband. Both appeared to be considering Maya's words.

"Mom, please. I need you to get well. You can't be tending to me instead of resting and making a quick recovery." She let go of her Mom's wrist and waited, mentally crossing her fingers. The last thing she wanted was to submit to her parent's ministrations, feeling more than ridiculous should they each attend to one of her feet as if she was in some kind of strange spa retreat.

Maya dragged her foot closer and pointed at the healed skin. "See? It's fine. Nothing a nice hot shower wouldn't help."

Leela gave a long sigh and nodded. She leaned forward and curled a lock of Maya's hair around her ear. "Okay, honey. If it's healed you may as well wash up. And I'll behave and go rest. But only because I'm feeling a little tired at the moment."

Maya stuck her tongue out at her mom and Leela laughed. It

was word for word the exact response Maya used to give when she finally acquiesced to her parent's instructions. She had to always make it seem like her choice.

As Leela walked to the door, Maya leaned against her pillows. Her heart was suddenly pounding rapidly as her vision filled with a memory of stone floors and the swaying of her body. She could feel the beat of the drums within her bones. Sabala whined loudly and Maya blinked, brought back to reality so quickly she felt bile rise in her throat.

Both her parents stopped in their tracks, Leela on the threshold, and Dev as he reached for the tray of towels. They glanced in unison at the hellhound, then at Maya.

She offered them an innocent smile which drew frowns from both of them, but they didn't press her for an explanation. Maya didn't miss the glance the couple shared so she knew they were more worried than they let on.

She waved her Mom off and sat there, watching her dad grab his kit and head out the door, thinking about the dream, she accepted how intense, how real it had been.

Could it have been a premonition?

Maya had never shown any sign of having the Sight. If she had, she'd have had some kind of manifestation of the ability so far. She'd always been disappointed she'd never had the odd gut instinct that warned her something was going to happen.

A déjà vu kind of vision, that instinctive reaction to catch something before it even began to fall. Or even the most convenient one, the itching hand to indicate the sudden influx of cash.

If she wasn't so exhausted, Maya would have been amused.

CHAPTER 7

$\mathcal{M}$AYA LAY ON her bed, staring at the ceiling.

She'd showered, washing off the dried blood and revealed the flushed pink skin on the newly knitted wounds. She'd been right. Nothing a little fire healing, and hot water couldn't cure.

Sabala watched her from his usual place at the foot of her bed.

She'd wondered what he'd been doing while she'd been dream-dancing around the house and bleeding her feet out?

Now, the hellhound's expression seemed to contain a tiny bit of guilt, and she wondered whether he'd been asleep on the job.

Not likely.

Yama, had given her the hellhound for a reason. He'd meant for the monstrous four-eyed dog to watch over her, but Sabala had done nothing to help in this particular instance.

It didn't matter anyway. It wasn't as if she'd been in any kind of serious danger.

She studied the dog fondly. Black velvety fur covered a lean muscular body, haunches as high as Maya's shoulders, and deadly sharp claws that sprang forth when required.

Maya's constant shadow was a demon dog, who'd hunted

down runaway Rakshasas who roamed the earth causing havoc among humans.

Guess body-guarding must get boring when compared to demon bounty-hunting.

A floorboard in the hall creaked, drawing both their attention to the open doorway.

Nik.

Nik scowled as he entered the room, his eyes, though impossibly black flared with sparks of amber.

Uh-oh.

He paused briefly to pat Sabala's head before sitting beside Maya. "I heard what happened. You certainly don't do things by half, do you?" A tight smile made a long line of his usually sexy lips and he shook his head as if he wasn't quite sure what to do with her.

As if trance dancing was her fault.

Maya ignored his stiffness and studied him, absorbing every detail of his dark hair and the way it brushed his shoulders, his broad well-muscled shoulders filling out his tan leather jacket, the dark navy of his Henley shirt and how it contrasted with his deep golden brown skin.

His voice brought her to attention. "What happened?"

"It's nothing. Just a little sleep dancing. I'm ok. No big deal."

"It's not nothing, Maya. You have no idea what you're dealing with here. It could have been dangerous. Could still be dangerous."

He paused, his skin dark now with anger, and worry.

She shook her head, trying to focus. "I told them they didn't need to call you. It wasn't really necessary. I'm fine." She spoke firmly to assure him she didn't need him.

Because that wasn't what their relationship was about.

Maya was no needy female.

Nik let out a frustrated grunt, and before she knew it he'd tugged her close to him and pressed an urgent kiss on her lips.

He'd been worried about her?

She had to admit having him concerned about her made her feel special. Wanted.

Not that she'd make him worry just because she felt like it. It was good to know he cared.

Now she allowed him to kiss her, smiled as his soft lips left a trail of heat in its wake as he deepened the kiss for a moment that turned out to be all too short. Then he was straightening and throwing a wary glance over his shoulder at the door.

The son of a god afraid of his girlfriend's father.

Cute?

Maya was still focused on him. His lips had made her mouth tingle, but despite the instinctive desire to pull him back toward her, Maya had things on her mind other than mindless kisses.

"I'm fine. I really am," she said softly, hoping her smile was convincing enough.

Sabala, having moved to a spot in front of the bedroom window, gave a very un-doglike snort. Clearly he didn't believe a word she said.

Maya chose to ignore him.

Nik said, "That's one of the things I adore about you. Crazy things happen and you just take it in your stride."

Maya grinned. He had a point. But her life recently had been all kinds of crazy. If she hadn't begun to adjust to the DEFCON 1 level of nuts that was her life, she probably would go out of her mind. "Welcome to my life."

Nik snorted as his phone buzzed.

Maya raised an eyebrow. His phone had been quiet for so long that any type of ringing drew her attention. Guess he was really back to work then.

Maya had to admit she felt a small disappointment in the pit of her stomach. Nik back at work meant Nik attending to drama all around the world. Which meant Nik not around very much.

She suppressed a sigh. This was who Nikhil was. She'd gone

into this with open eyes. And if she wanted it to work with him she had to use a good dose more maturity than most people her age. Nik was never without his phone, and Maya understood all too well his responsibilities.

Not long ago they'd come to terms with the fact that there would be nothing normal about their relationship. As hard as it had been to adapt to a boyfriend who flitted across the world to deal with mythical, magical and mortal transgressions, Maya had learned to accept it. And be happy with it.

Now, she watched as Nik withdrew his smartphone from his jeans pocket, studied the screen then stowed the device. Nik shifted his attention to Maya. Apparently, whatever it was wasn't as important as her.

Sometimes Nik could be so sensitive and sweet.

"So. Tell me exactly what happened in your dream," he asked.

He was back to business, and it calmed Maya. She relayed her dream, everything from the abandoned temple and old stone carvings, to the beating of the drum and the intense energy of the dance.

When she ended with the golden light and the fact that she'd passed out exhausted and bleeding from the effort of the dance, Nik's eyebrows rose.

He pursed his lips, mulling over what she'd recounted. "Let me do some investigating. I have an odd feeling this sounds familiar."

"Familiar?" Maya frowned, her stomach churning again. Familiar meant this horror had happened to someone in real life and Maya was not ready to hear that. "Familiar in what way?"

Nik shrugged. "Something I saw come through my emails. I haven't been assigned to anything in a while but I still get blind copied on all communications. I have a feeling I've read something similar to this in an email a while ago. But . . . this could just as easily have been a bad dream." He paused as if he wanted to say something more but thought it best to remain silent.

"But?" probed Maya.

Nik rubbed the back of his neck. "But there is a chance you're channeling the thoughts of someone else."

Cold fear wash over Maya. "You mean I could be seeing something that's actually happening?"

Nik nodded, looking worried.

"Crap."

CHAPTER 8

"DO YOU REALLY THINK it could be the Sight?" Maya asked.

He frowned. "It's entirely possible. But I have to look into it before I make any assumptions. If the Mother Kali gave you the power of foresight, I'm sure she will be happy to confirm."

Maya nodded solemnly. She'd summon the goddess herself if it would answer her questions.

Nik got to his feet and began to pace. "Thing is, you could just as likely be seeing what's happening right now, experiencing what someone else is experiencing in the moment."

"The dreams could be real."

Nik nodded. "It's possible."

She shook her head and glared at him. "What are you not telling me? I can hear it in your voice. You're worried about something." Even Sabala huffed, as if to agree with her.

Nik let out a sigh, and slowly came to sit beside her again, as if reluctant to reveal more. Finally he met her gaze. "If you hacked into the thoughts and experiences of a real person, then we need to find out who she is and where she is."

Maya sucked in her breath.

"We have to find her," he said softly.

Maya now understood his meaning. What she'd felt and seen would have been far worse in reality, far worse for the girl who'd experienced the horror first hand. If Maya's feet had bled, who knew what the poor dancer had endured, wherever she was right now.

If she was experiencing anything and not dead.

Was she seriously entertaining the possibility that her vision was real?

But she had to.

A girl's life might be at stake.

"If this is . . . real," she asked Nik, "then why would someone dance and dance until her feet bleed and she collapses and passes out?"

Nik's eyes were shadowed, worry darkening them. "I'm not sure." If he was worried, then that made Maya worried. "Anything else you saw that you may have forgotten to tell me?"

Maya's brow creased as she ran through what she was able to recall from the dream. "There was the statue."

"What statue?"

"The Nataraja. It was made of stone. But towards the end of the dream it began to glow as if it was on fire. And it seemed to be the same glow I saw at the edges of my vision. It felt like a strange energy taking over me."

"Did it feel like the energy was inside you? Or around you?"

Maya thought for a moment before saying, "To be honest it felt like both." She leaned back against the pillows as all her energy finally drained out of her body. "It felt like the dancing was creating an energy inside me, and then, when I saw the glow, it seemed like there was more energy around my body. Or rather, the dancer's body."

Nik shifted closer, his finger tapping on his watch over and over. "Did the energy feel the same? You were generating the power from inside of your body? Were you also drawing energy from the outside?"

She nodded, understanding what he was asking. "Yes. And the energy felt the same. It felt as if the dancing was creating some kind of strange power, and then that power was seeping out of my body and filling the air around me."

"And that energy was making the statue glow?"

"I can't be certain of that. I wasn't aware of when the statue began to glow. So it *is* possible the dancer's energy was feeding power to the statue." Maya stared at Nik, shocked. "That's insane. Can such a thing really happen?"

Nik nodded. "All sorts of devotion create power. That's why your parents initially thought . . . that your experience was a trance. When a devotee loses themselves within their devotion, it creates an energy that channels the god. In this case, it's possible the dancer's energy created a channel to Lord Nataraja. Any god would have felt that power and come to her."

But Maya was shaking her head. "But it didn't feel like a god. I would have assumed that if Nataraja was coming to his devotee, a dancer who was dancing with such extreme passion, that he would be benevolent, loving. But what I felt wasn't anything like benevolence."

Sabala clacked across the floor and nudged her knee with his nose. Maya ran her fingers over his head, glad for the comfort.

Nik frowned. "Okay. I'd rather not make assumptions right now. Let me look into it and get back to you. In the meantime, get some rest." He was beginning to take on that bossy tone. The one that said he expected her to obey.

But Maya wasn't planning to. "There's nothing wrong with me. I was just channeling the dancer. Whatever happened to her didn't happen to me."

Nik groaned. "You ever listen to anybody? Did you see the condition of your feet?"

He leaned over and pulled the covers off of Maya's feet and

stared at her soles. She knew what he was seeing. The bottoms of her feet were black and blue, still bruised, even after the fire treatment. She'd only been able to do so much. The rest of the healing process would be a combination of her own body, and a few sessions of added fire to hurry things along.

He pointed at her feet. "This look like nothing to you?"

It still looked like a hot mess. Even Maya could see that. So there was nothing she could say in response. He had a damn good point.

Besides, even if she was stupid enough to argue with him, it wasn't as if she could get out of the bed right now and take a walk. Her feet throbbed, the injuries burned like hell, the tissue infused with fire, still regenerating.

Pity all this was caused by the fact that Maya had been dancing.

The truth of the matter was she'd always wanted to dance. She'd just never been coordinated. The movements and sequences had been incredibly hard for her to master.

The memory of dancing in the dream, of her body moving to the beautiful beat of the drum, had been quite entrancing. And strangely, she longed to dance again.

Nik cleared his throat beside her, bringing her attention back to him. She blinked.

She'd forgotten he was there.

Sabala bobbed his head beneath her fingers, reminding her he too was there, wondering where she'd gone.

Nik scowled and stared at her face. "What's wrong?" He peered into her eyes as if her pupils would give him the answer.

She hesitated only a moment before deciding *what the hell.* "I'm not sure. It's the strangest thing. I feel like I want to dance again . . . but I can't dance. Not really."

Nik took her free hand, folding his own fingers over hers. "I want you to promise me you will not get up until I return."

Maya gave him a thin smile and a nod, her spine stiffening

subtly. She was fine. Her feet would be fine in a few hours, all back to normal. Why was it nobody understood that with Kali's healing fire she was as good as new?

Now, she forced herself to keep her annoyance off her face, because despite her irritation she was well aware that everyone around her had her best interests at heart. How could she fight with them when they cared?

Nik's eyes narrowed as he said, "I'll go and look into this and I'll return straightaway. Your life could be in danger. Whatever happened to the girl, you channeled it today. Whatever is causing this, whether it be deific, demonic, or human, it's dark. And dangerous. The very fact that you were there, however intangible the experience, may well provide that darkness with a passage, a way to come to you. Whatever compulsion you feel to dance again, don't give in."

He was no longer kidding.

It all sounded so ominous, but Maya nodded solemnly and promised to obey.

"I'll be back soon."

He didn't stick around for small talk. But he did pause and give her a warning glare. As if he thought the moment he left she'd jump off the bed and dance until sunrise.

Nik disappeared.

As a demigod, Nik had lived a long time. Would live a long time more. Probably forever if he was never mortally injured.

That bothered Maya a great deal but she tried not to think about it too much. For now, she took every day as it came, and enjoyed her relationship with Nik for what it was.

A mutual attraction, a shared devotion to each other. And a whole lot of respect. Something she'd always thought necessary in any relationship.

As exhaustion pulled at her, Maya fell asleep with a smile on her face.

CHAPTER 9

MAYA WOKE a little later, her arm being jerked left and right. At the end of her arm was Joss, looming over her, her eyes concerned.

The scent of mac-and-cheese drifted towards Maya's nostrils and she grinned.

"Lunchtime. I'm just dropping in to make sure you eat this." Joss's tone was firm.

"Lunchtime?" Maya asked, groggy as she shifted her gaze to her open window. Sunlight filled the room but no shadows were cast on the brightly patterned carpet.

At least midday from the looks of it.

Sabala was sitting in the corner beside the window, watching Joss and Maya, his expression almost amused. The hellhound and Joss had reached an uneasy truce, which Maya prayed would last.

Right now, Joss was ignoring him. And he her.

Joss snorted. "Next time you dance the night away, please take me along. I'm not sure you know what you're doing." She waved at the food. "Boss says you need to eat."

Maya scooted up in the bed and leaned against the headboard

with the pillows behind her. "You won't have me complaining. Especially since you come bearing that divine dish."

Joss laughed. "Who doesn't love mac and cheese?" Maya's nightstand contained two bowls and two glasses of OJ on a wooden tray. Sabala's short sniff drew Maya's attention and she met his gaze. The fact that the hellhound never ate had always struck Maya as strange, but then he was a demonic creature. So what was with his look? Did he suddenly have a hankering for mac and cheese?

Joss handed her a bowl, took the other for herself and the two girls ate in silence. Even Joss, who was usually the one who talked with her mouth full, and waved her fork around like crazy as she spoke. Not that she lacked manners. Just that remaining silent for too long was not Joss's strong-suit.

Maya knew Joss just as well as she knew Ria Gupta, the third - and very absent - member of their little group. Right now, neither of the girls knew where Ria was, and both couldn't wait until it was safe to see her again. Weeks had passed since Ria had gone into hiding, assisted by Maya's parents and the agency in escaping her abusive fiancé.

Neither Joss nor Maya spoke much about Ria, yet both missed her like crazy. And worried about her more. Ria would be worse than Joss had she been here right this minute.

Joss cleared her throat. "So how do you feel?" she asked, leaning forward as she chewed. "Do your feet feel any better?"

Maya nodded, the pasta having taken the edge off her hunger. Strangely enough, as soon as she'd smelled the food she'd been hit by a ravenous desire for sustenance. As if she hadn't eaten in weeks.

"Better. So hungry, which is weird. You have perfect timing."

Joss smiled. "It's just a short visit. There's some crazy shit happening right now. I'll head out soon to help your dad with a case."

Maya raised her eyebrows, curious. "What case?"

Such was their life these days. They spent most of their time in the field on cases. When not working they studied, both plodding along at their own pace to get through their final high school year. With neither of them having a set-in-stone deadline as to college entry, they just got what needed to be completed done, and then moved on to the next.

Some weeks were frenetic, filled with cases, others quiet and filled with schoolwork.

Joss shook her head, then pointed her fork at Maya. "You just mind your own business and concentrate on healing."

Wrinkling her eyebrows, Maya groaned, "Come on Joss, all I'm asking for is information. Besides, it's not as if I'm still hurt. I did heal myself you know." A ripple of guilt ran through Maya and she shifted her gaze to her food. Her limbs tensed, her heart thudding as if expecting the music to play.

She stiffened.

Was that music she just heard? A Staccato beat that implied an impending increase in tempo. Maya's entire body strained to hear more but she shoved the urge down, buried it as deep as she could.

The need to dance had come back with full force and Maya blinked hard and forced herself to concentrate.

Joss sighed and shovelled the last bite of pasta into her mouth. After swallowing, she said, "Fine. Strictly to satisfy your curiosity." She glared at Maya, her warning clear. "There's been an issue with zombies in the downtown LA area."

"Zombies?" Maya frowned.

Only a few weeks ago, Narakasura, the Rakshasa king reborn - or Kas as Maya had known him - had imprisoned Lord Yama, and the world had been overrun with the living dead. The Walking Dead was nothing compared to downtown LA three weeks past.

In the end, Kas had been killed and the god of the dead had been released, restoring order to the world.

"I thought the undead problem had been solved after Yama was freed." Maya reached for her OJ and sipped.

Joss nodded, getting to her feet, all businesslike. "That's what we'd all thought. But everyone admits it's not a perfect system. Apparently a few managed to slip under the radar. KALIMA is still not sure how they managed it. Evading the big man downstairs is not an easy feat."

Maya smiled.

Only Joss would come up with descriptions like those and be totally unrepentant. Maya had a feeling Lord Yama would find it amusing - should he hear her friend speak.

"Your dad asked me to come with him. Something about gaining more field experience." She grabbed her juice and downed it in one long swallow, clearly in a hurry.

Maya nodded.

With all the mayhem of the last few months, Joss had convinced Dev to allow her to join KALIMA - the organization Maya's parents had helped to set up. An organization dedicated to ridding the world and its occupants of a plethora of demons and evil. Gone were the days when people just prayed and hoped for the evil creatures to go away.

These days people called KALIMA. Through temples and priests, friends and neighbors, the Kali agents were a worldwide initiative the Winchesters would have been proud of.

Joss's parents had returned for a brief period, having been grounded post Rise of the Living Dead. They'd checked in on Joss, said all the right things, then departed in a flurry of cordial politeness leaving the Raos, and their newly appropriated daughter Joss, a little shell-shocked.

They'd been satisfied Maya's parents would look after their child, and had set up a bank account for her expenses. Before leaving Joss's mother had taken Leela aside, their conversation longer than any they'd had since they'd met.

Leela had never divulged what they'd discussed. And Maya had been too afraid to probe.

Joss had accepted the impending absence of her parents with customary cheer, and had adjusted well to being an adopted Rao.

Maya was glad to be there for her friend. Though Joss was a bit of a rebel, Maya preferred not to think about what her friend would have done had she been alone, without support.

Joss had the tendency to go a little wild, although she'd toned it down a good few notches after her last drinking binge had almost gotten Maya attacked, and ended up with Maya barbecuing a Rakshasa demon - who wasn't supposed to exist - and meeting a real-life demigod - who was definitely not supposed to exist.

Joss's situation was strange and sad. Thanks to her father's lucrative stockbroking business, her parents travelled the world regularly. A lot. They were of the assumption that their daughter was extremely independent, and never once thought she'd like to join them.

In all the years Maya had known Joss, she could count on one hand the number of times she'd met Joss's mother in the flesh. On more than one occasion, Maya had been tempted to give the woman a piece of her mind.

But, out of respect for Joss, she'd held her tongue.

Right now, Dev was including Joss in the case, keeping her attention off the absence of her parents. With their studies keeping them on their toes, forcing them to juggle their time between school and supernatural investigations, things were certainly interesting.

"I'm coming," said Maya, putting her bowl on her nightstand and shimmying to the edge of the mattress.

"The hell you are," said Joss, her voice breaking on a squeak of anger. "Had I known you'd insist on coming, I never would've told you. You're meant to be resting. Do you really think you're able to go anywhere with those feet?"

Joss had a point but she'd forgotten Maya could heal herself.

Maya folded her arms and glared at her friend. "I'm perfectly capable of coming with you. I *am* already healing."

Joss shrugged. "That's beside the point. Even Nik said you are not to leave your bed until he drops by. You promised. The last thing I want is to be in trouble with a god."

Maya rolled her eyes. "As if you're afraid of Nik."

Joss was a total fan of Nik, both as a demigod and as Maya's boyfriend. And she was taking his side, glaring at Maya with disapproval.

"I don't need to be afraid of Nik to know what he's saying makes sense. Whatever you just experienced, it's definitely some weird shit. You have any idea how worried your parents are? You danced until your feet bled. Not something that happens every day."

Maya shook her head. "Don't you think I'm well aware of that?"

Joss raised an eyebrow. "You don't seem to be. Especially when you're busy demanding to go out on a case when you're still not well."

"But I'm fine." Maya spoke firmly. "And this is my job. My responsibility. I can't let-"

Joss lifted her fork and pointed it at Maya. "We all have a responsibility in this. Just because *you* have special godly-imbued powers doesn't mean *you* are more responsible for anything. Your parents have been doing this way longer then you. They've got this."

Maya snorted and leaned back.

Joss wasn't the only person in Maya's life who thought it was their duty to boss her around. Her mom's bestie, Claudia Romero, would have also been in her face about taking care of herself. At least, she would have until Maya's actions had rendered her unable to walk again.

Maya brushed away the stab of sadness and focused on Joss as she put her bowl beside Maya's. "Now, I suggest you rest up. Your mom said to tell you she'd be up in about an hour to check on you."

Maya nodded. She'd come to accept that arguing with Joss was a waste of time. So she let her friend believe she was going to behave herself and stay in bed. Sabala whuffed. Was he warning Joss? The traitor.

Joss glanced at the hellhound then gave Maya a suspicious glare, but she didn't question Maya any further. She rose and gathered the dishes before heading out of the room. At the doorway she turned back and gave Maya a warning glare. "I mean it. You stay right there and get better."

Then she was gone.

CHAPTER 10

MAYA THREW BACK the bedclothes and drew her feet towards her. Sabala tilted his head as he watched her, probably already suspecting what she intended to do.

The hellhound was smart that way.

But even he would understand Maya's need to help. It wasn't as if she was so damaged she couldn't handle one case. If she was a narcoleptic then she may have been worried about sleep-dancing while on the job. Thankfully, she wasn't.

She changed from her pajamas into a pair of jeans and a sweatshirt before searching out the softest pair of socks she owned. Her feet were swollen and she knew before she even tried, that her favorite boots wouldn't fit.

She retrieved an old pair of hiking boots from the back of her closet. Her mom had insisted she buy one size larger, because apparently hiking up mountains swelled one's feet. Not that she'd ever used the boots for hiking.

She laced them and got to her feet before rummaging in her closet for her satchel. It still contained her Madus, the poison that went with it, and a couple of small daggers she'd been training with. Along with a first aid kit and a change of clothes, her satchel was an official go-bag.

Throwing her cellphone into the satchel, she slung it over her shoulder and headed out the door. The clicking on the wood floor confirmed Sabala followed closely. Maya didn't have much of a choice.

Not as if she could get rid of the hellhound.

Besides, taking him with would get her in a little less trouble with Nik. Being partially responsible and taking her guard dog with her may get Nik to cut her some slack. The operative word being *may*.

She headed down the stairs to her dad's study where she slid in behind his desk and swiped a finger across the trackpad of his Mac. The screen glowed with a request for password and she quickly tapped it in.

Her dad had given her her own set of passwords to access the computer, making it clear they kept no secrets from her. Not to mention sometimes, when he wasn't at home, new cases would arise. Over the last few months she'd become increasingly active in attending to cases without him. It filled her with pride to know he trusted her that much.

But, right now, as she scrolled through his emails and read the very last one, she felt a stab of guilt. He wouldn't be happy with her. She was disobeying both his and Nik's instructions but she was prepared to take the heat.

If I saved his life, he'd get over it.

Besides, Maya was really fine. Why did everyone want to coddle her as if she was made of fragile crystal or something?

Probably a good thing Claudia wasn't here to nag her into submission too. She'd been acting strangely these past few weeks which had ratcheted up Maya's guilt. There were times when she'd seen anger, and fear, in her aunt's eyes and Maya had been tempted to visit with her to help ease her pain.

But Claudia had kept them all at a distance. Her aunt had

been her confidante for most of her lifetime, and even in recent weeks when the rift between them had widened, Maya knew that given the chance, Claude would come down on her like a ton of bricks if she ended up injured.

But they had to understand. Maya had powers given to her for a reason. What was the point in being powerful, having the ability to heal herself, if she was treated like a fragile Faberge egg every time she was injured. They had to come to terms with the fact that she was more resilient than a normal human.

The last email from KALIMA headquarters detailed a downtown LA location that was well known for its homeless population. Known locally as the Lower Waterfront, the squatter community was located beneath the new Everson Overpass as it ran over Murphy's River near the harbor.

After Kas's efforts to cheat death, that part of LA had been overrun with the undead. It had taken a combination of Lord Yama's efforts, plus that of the local police, to clean up the area.

Maya nodded to herself, then headed for the door when the sound of music filled her ears. Maya stiffened, holding her breath and waiting. Was it happening again? Her fingers fisted around the shoulder strap of her satchel as her muscled tightened, as her body seemed to want to move against her will, pulled by some invisible force.

She wanted to dance.

But Nik had said to resist. She couldn't give in. She just couldn't allow herself to be drawn into a trance from which she was unable to awaken.

She inhaled sharply and straightened, focusing on the room, her breathing, and what she was supposed to do. If this continued to happen she was definitely going to have a talk with Kali.

She wasn't sure where her mom was, or if she was inside the house, and hoped she wouldn't hear Maya leave.

Maya would be hard pressed to find a way to convince her

Mom to allow her to go. Leela could be pretty terrifying when she wanted.

But she managed to grab her car keys and lock the front door without alerting her.

Maya scrambled into her ancient Mini and rolled out of the drive without looking back, and made the journey to LA as fast as she could while still sticking to frustratingly slow speed limits. Now, more than ever, she wished she had either the goddess Chayya with her, or Nik, to transport her there with ease.

She glanced at Sabala, who sat beside her, his expression indignant. She supposed she could've asked him to take her since, with his teleportation powers, he was perfectly capable, but she wasn't confident enough.

He'd more likely take her directly back home. Or worse, to Patala where she'd remain under lock and key until she healed.

So she drove.

DOWNTOWN LA HELD an air of desertion.

Ghost town, much.

Maya turned towards Murphy's River as it ran along the edge of the harbor's eastern border. The Waterfront community had settled beneath the overpass, erecting homes so makeshift all it would take was a cart and two minutes of packing to haul it away.

Maya parked as close to the river as possible. She didn't care about her car being stolen as Sabala had already thrown a glamor over it and hidden the vehicle from passers-by. She still locked it, though, and Sabala followed as she headed towards the overpass.

Cardboard boxes provided temporarily permanent shelter to dozens of homeless. Maya even spotted a few requisite shopping carts piled with trash.

As she picked a path along the river, she felt the prickle of pain in the bottom of her feet. The entire drive her foot had throbbed as she'd pressed the accelerator.

Now she paused, studying the homes, watching an old man shuffle by. His limp hair had greyed, not salt-and-pepper but dirty stained off-white that cried out for a good shampoo. The poor man was hunched over, spine was so curved she couldn't understand how he managed to move at all. And yet he did, his jacket and pants, so faded that barely a hint remained of the original color of the garment.

Nondescript hair and clothes for a nondescript life.

He stared suspiciously at Maya as he limped past, the front of his shoes flapping open with a loud slap, revealing his soiled toes, and ingrown toenails now thick and hard from lack of care. He slapped his way loudly past her, and she looked over her shoulder and studied him for a while, but he appeared to be of no threat.

With Sabala at her side, people usually avoided her, pushed away by the negative energy of the hellhound. Humans registered demonic vibes on some unconscious level.

She watched the line of shacks and pulled fire to her feet for added healing energy. The burst of warmth helped ease the throbbing and she felt a little bit more confident.

She had no fear about defending herself. But her fire was extremely powerful and she worried she'd probably be a danger to innocents around her if things went sideways.

Maya flared her nostrils, and scented the air. The water from the river flowed by slowly and stank of urine, and other unidentifiable odors. Beyond that, the odor of unwashed bodies drifted towards her, almost overpowering.

The city council had been proactive in the last few weeks; they'd set up portable shower units all across the poorest parts of the city in the hope that the homeless would use them. Of course, when it had first been put up, there had been a certain amount of interest. But now, both interest and curiosity had waned.

Maya had no illusions about homelessness. She knew people suffered both on a financial as well as an emotional level. She knew too that if she dug deeper, each and every one of the people who lived along the river would have a history that would bring tears to her eyes.

The mentally challenged, the abused, the drug addicted, the financially insolvent, so many people without homes, without people who cared for them enough to ensure they didn't end up on the streets.

Maya swallowed hard, as hot emotions began to rise within her. She hated that they had to live like this. And wished more than once she had the kind of financial backing that would allow her to help these people. Even if it was to just set up a soup kitchen to provide meals for them every day.

She took a deep breath and hurried forward, looking for her father. Sooner or later she was going to have to face the music from various parties. Which made her wonder why one particular party hadn't come back to her on what he'd found out. She sure hoped Nik had something concrete to tell her when he finally did show.

The scent on the air confirmed both he and Joss had passed by not too long ago. Beside her, Sabala sniffed the air with what Maya assumed was an expression of recognition.

They were somewhere deep within the shadows beneath the bridge, inspecting the little tents and cardboard caves, and looking for the undead.

Beyond the distinct bad hygiene, even beyond the familiar smell of her family, Maya had already detected the odor of rotten meat.

She'd long since become acclimated to the smell of Demons. Raw meat or rotting flesh, and spices, which had seemed strange at first, to be connected directly to Demon or Rakshasa.

In the aftermath of Kas's epidemic of the undead, Maya had discovered that the people who had died but hadn't died, had also taken on an odor similar to the rakshasa.

Similar, but not the same.

And now, all she had to do was follow her nose.

Oh, and refuse to give in to the call of the music should it attempt to entrance her again. Maya swallowed hard as she walked slowly, the rough heels of her hiking boots echoing on the concrete floor as she passed one haphazardly constructed lean-to after another. Faces peered at her, features hidden by grime, clothing dirty and discolored. Discarded takeout containers, bottles empty of alcohol and other beverages, food wrappers and boxes. The further she went the more her heart hurt.

She forced herself to concentrate on the smell, taking one step after another and following the stench. It annoyed her now; her dad knew she had the ability to easily smell the undead, and yet he'd thought it better to leave her at home.

She'd have been happy to come and help, even if they had to wheel her out here in a wheelchair. It would certainly have saved him a lot of wasted time. Considering she'd caught up to him, she knew she was right.

The smell was strong now, and Maya slowly came to a stop. Against the back edge of the overhanging bridge, she made out a lean-to constructed from a combination of foam, cardboard and bubblewrap.

She smelled someone inside.

Sabala snuffed, as if trying not to sneeze.

Maya's heart began to beat faster. Then she flinched as someone lurched towards her, yelling words, thankfully unintelligible. She took a step away, then glanced around.

An old woman, her dark matted hair hanging on either side of her lined face, was advancing on her, waving an old shoe in Maya's direction.

Maya raised a hand, placating the woman.

"It's okay. I don't want to hurt you. I'm just looking."

Maya spoke in a rush, trying to get the words out before the shoe landed on her head. Before Sabala, who'd already bared his teeth to the woman, decided she was a threat to Maya. Besides, it was important she stood her ground, or she'd never win the woman over.

But it didn't seem to be a problem.

The woman muttered something under her breath, waved the shoe in Maya's face once more, and turned and ambled off into the darkness. Maya shook her head as Sabala's breathing returned to normal.

Thanks pooch.

She'd been so ready to talk the woman down she felt slightly off kilter as her heart returned to it's normal pace.

She took a step closer to the sleeping man. Here the smell was stronger, almost overpowering enough that Maya was tempted to put her hand over her nose.

Bad idea.

Firstly, it would be an insult to the people around here should she reveal that the smell affected her.

Secondly, it wasn't as if hiding her face would stop her smelling the odor. She was detecting the essence of the demon rather than their physical smell.

She sank to her knees in front of a piece of hanging cardboard, pushing it aside to peer into the darkness. Sabala remained a few feet away, as if implying this wasn't what he'd signed up for.

A glance over her shoulder and Maya was relieved to find no-one, other than the cranky old woman, was paying much attention to her. She drew a tiny bit of fire into the palm of her hand and stuck it inside the dark interior of the tent.

The small ball lit the space and shone on the face of the man.

Maya startled, flinching so hard her fire sputtered out and she ended up landing on her ass.

She struggled to get back to her feet and tried to bring her breathing back to normal. She hadn't expected to see a corpse so desiccated it looked not much better than the ancient mummies of Egypt.

The undead caused by Yama's disappearance had been people

who'd died just before the god was removed from his role. His absence had imbued them with a strange kind of life.

Yama had reappeared though, and as he'd been restored, many of the not-dead dead had just fallen back to death.

And, physically, they hadn't looked all that different.

Decomposition had halted, so when the proper death had been restored, bodies hadn't exploded in a hot mess, nor had they disintegrated into a neat pile of dust easily swept away.

Not so for the man she now stared at. His skin was brown, leathery. His eyes sunken into his eye sockets. The odor inside the tent was overpowering. Maya sat back on her heels. She couldn't be of any help to him.

He was gone. A mystery as to what had killed him, but he was dead.

Maya got to her feet, turned, and walked straight into her dad's chest.

"What the hell are you doing here?" asked Dev. He kept his voice low, though she could still hear his fury. Could see it pretty clearly in his eyes.

Maya glared at Sabala.

Thanks for the heads up, hellhound.

She straightened and replied, "Had to come and help." She lifted her chin and met his eyes defiantly. She was ready for the telling off that would come. Then again, maybe she wasn't, because the next thing out of her mouth was a redirection of his attention. "I found something back there." She pointed a thumb over her shoulder at the tent.

She stood aside, allowing her father to crouch and peer into the tent. He pointed a flashlight inside, bringing the mummy-like face of the man into stark contrast.

Dev got to his feet and sighed. He looked at Maya. "Any ideas what could have done that?"

Maya shook her head. "He looks mummified. Something,

whatever it is that killed him, sucked out every bit of moisture from his body."

Dev nodded. He'd already gathered as much. He retrieved his phone, proceeded to call headquarters and request a backup team, his anger controlled, yet tangible.

Uh-oh.

CHAPTER 12

*D*EV RANG OFF and slid his phone back into his jeans pocket. As he moved, his jacket shifted to reveal the revolver strapped to his torso. Maya raised her eyebrows.

What good would a weapon like that do against the supernatural creatures he dealt with?

Her dad's lip curled in amusement. "You don't have to look at me that way. I'm not stupid enough to bring a weapon with normal human ammunition to this kind of gunfight." Maya shook her head but her father continued, waving her into silence. "We've been working on some ammunition. Holy water and frankincense and copper et cetera. It's all very interesting."

"And very weird." Maya grinned.

Dev let out a short laugh. Was he beginning to forget he was supposed to be angry with Maya? "So we'll have a team down here within the next ten minutes. We should get going."

Maya was only too happy to leave. Turning on her heel, she followed her father who'd already began to walk off. Joss remained at her side, although her friend was silent. Something was on her mind, but this wasn't exactly the place to talk about it.

Sabala clicked behind them as they headed off. They were

beginning to attract more attention from the residents. Maya found she was unconsciously stepping up the pace as she imagined the residents becoming violent in response to their trespassing.

Paranoid much.

She was not afraid of them. She was just afraid of what she would end up doing to them if she was forced to defend herself with her fire.

As they hurried past the long line of cardboard homes, Maya stopped in her tracks so suddenly that Joss was already ten feet ahead before she realized she was alone.

She turned and stared at Maya and the hellhound, who'd also stopped.

Joss already knew that when Maya behaved oddly, like now, something was usually wrong. She didn't ask any questions, just hurried back to Maya and waited at her side.

In the distance, Maya could see her father slowing down too. He turned and watched them, curious now as he waited. Maya was glad he didn't come running back to her. She wasn't in the mood to be crowded.

She used her nose again, scenting for that particular odor that had caught her attention. It, too, smelled like a demon. The rotting flesh, the spices, this time it wasn't so strong. It was more of a hint than a pungent perfume.

"I think I smell another one."

Sabala whuffed, confirming it, while Joss stared in the direction of the glamored animal. She hated when he went invisible.

Problem was, Maya was a little uncertain of what exactly she was smelling. If she had to compare it with the odor of the desiccated corpse they'd just discovered, she'd say it was either rakshasa or an undead who was still alive.

Maya preferred the undead.

She followed the smell. It wasn't easy, as the odor was faint. The ammonia from the river was strong here and it would be strong enough to hide the scent of an undead unless you were blessed with a timely breeze. Which explained why Maya hadn't caught it the first time she'd gone by.

They passed a small shack made of rubber sheeting and a couple of broken shipping pallets. Within the shadows of the room, beneath a blanket, Maya could make out an unmoving form.

With Sabala at her elbow, she sank to her haunches and peered inside, her nose telling her she'd found her quarry. Her heart pumped hard in her chest, as she worried about what she was going to see. Finding the desiccated corpse of the previous zombie had not been an enjoyable experience, and Maya wasn't looking forward to going in for round two.

She stuck her hand inside the tent, and drew fire to the palm of her hand. She kept it subtle, so as not to frighten the person, but she needn't have worried. The woman was fast asleep, her gaunt face skeletonized by the shadows. Her skin was pasty pale, her lips black. Easy signs to identify her as an undead. Another one that had slipped under the radar, lost in the search that had rounded up so many of them during the past few months.

And undead she was, sleeping peacefully in this little community of homeless people.

Within the tiny quarters, Maya made out little more than just her sleeping pallet. It made sense she had no food cartons.

The undead did not eat. Once they were resurrected, food was the last thing they wanted. What they sought out for sustenance did not need to be cooked.

Just like the fictional zombies, the undead fed on blood. Whether it be directly from the vein of a living being, or from a freshly killed human. Blood was their sustenance.

These were the modern versions of vampires. Of course, they came without the ability to transport themselves from place to place, or turning into bats and flying off into the night.

But the closest thing Maya had ever seen to that kind of

undead was the Vitala, a vampire type demon Maya had fought before. She glanced at Joss and they both got to their feet. Maya tilted her head in her father's direction and Joss took off, bringing him back as discreetly as she could. Being the head of their outfit, and the fact that he was on-scene, he'd have to be the one to verify the find.

Even in their shadow organization there were rules.

Maya could see the concern, combined with excitement, in her friend's eyes. Joss was also afraid of what the undead could do. Many people, innocents, cops, and Yama's agents, had died trying to apprehend them.

And from what Maya was seeing now, many more people would, unless they found a way to bring the undead in safely.

Dev paused at the entrance to the tent as Sabala shifted aside, met Maya's eyes, and received a short nod. She remained where she was as he rushed off to make the call a little distance from the tent.

No sense in causing a riot among the residents.

He'd be calling headquarters again, and requesting more an evacuation team for the bodies.

This case had been more than successful. They'd found a dead zombie, one whose death seemed inexplicable. And they'd also found one alive. Two undead so well hidden for all these months.

Goes to show, how few people truly see the homeless.

Even those who claim they're aware, that they respect these people, even those who open their wallets and donate towards their well-being, didn't really see them. Too few people would truly sacrifice to give the homeless a helping hand.

Here in the Waterfront community, it would have been easy for the two zombies to stay hidden, within this population of the unseen.

Maya remained outside of the tent, watching the woman breathe. That she made use of her lungs even though she was technically dead, was not only an automatic nervous system glitch. It was understood that even the undead required some form of cell oxygenation in order to remain 'alive'.

Oily strands of dark hair surrounded her face, squashed beneath a multicolored beanie. Her body was hidden beneath layers of clothing, at least three jackets and two pairs of pants. Had she been trying to blend in with the rest of the community? As far as Maya knew the undead weren't affected by the weather.

Footsteps and the grating of gurney wheels on concrete drifted towards Maya. The team had arrived to remove the body, and she was not surprised to see two agents attired in hazmat suits shuffling towards her.

They paid no attention to her, just pushed their gurney along and headed straight for Dev who led them toward the shack in which Maya had found the undead male.

Maya stiffened, keeping an eye on the sleeping zombie. The woman shifted on the pallet, and shuddered, pulling the blanket closer. Maya frowned and leaned in, recognizing the beads of sweat covering the undead's forehead. When she began to cough softly, Maya frowned, confused.

A sick undead?

Things just kept getting weirder and weirder. How the hell did an undead get sick? Maya's heart tightened.

Who was this woman?

The hazmat suits and gurney trundled past, taking the other undead away. Her focus was the sleeping woman, who was so deeply unconscious she didn't even know what was happening around her.

A few of the homeless had gathered to watch the activity. Many were pointing and whispering, and Maya could understand the sight of hazmat suits would be far from comforting.

She didn't have to wait long before the team returned, bringing a second gurney straight for the woman's tent. Maya stood aside as they leaned in and grabbed a hold of the sleeping bag.

"Be careful," Maya said, her voice filled with warning. "She isn't dead."

One of the hazmats turned to look at her, and she made out a pair of startled blue eyes behind the thick glass of his helmet.

She couldn't determine the expression, but she said, "She does look like she is sick."

The guy's eyebrows rose.

Maya nodded, understanding his disbelief. "She is sick. She's got a fever and a slight cough. And she's sleeping really deeply, so I'm assuming she's either unconscious or in some kind of coma."

His expression remained skeptical and Maya could well understand it. Undead illness was unheard of, as far as Maya was aware. Which begged the question: What the heck was wrong with this particular zombie?

The agent nodded, then leaned inside to say something to his partner who was already kneeling beside the woman's head. They were much more gentle with her now, sliding her out and carrying her carefully to the gurney, although Maya had to wonder if their tenderness had more to do with ensuring they didn't upset her because she'd probably go nuts, try to defend herself, and injure them in the process.

Still smart.

Maya followed, Sabala a few steps behind, a still silent Joss at her side. They watched as the agents wheeled the woman to the ambulance. Maya stood a few feet from her still invisible car, her arms wrapped around her body, and watched as her father coordinated the bagging and tagging of both the zombies, living and dead.

When the ambulance sped off in silence, only its red lights flashing, Dev turned to her and said, "Meet me at the medical centre." His tone was curt.

So he was still pissed off at her.

He turned on his heel and headed for his car, leaving the two girls watching as he drove off.

Maya was ready for the sounding off she knew was coming. What she couldn't wait for was to hear what Nik had found out. As much as Maya was feeling useful right now, she was still frustrated at how little understanding she had about the dream and what it meant.

The only good thing was she hadn't felt the compulsion to dance in the last hour. Who knew how long that would last?

Maya turned to Joss. "Need a ride?"

Sabala dropped the glamor and revealed the hidden blue Mini.

Staring at the suddenly visible car, Joss snorted and headed for the passenger door.

CHAPTER 13

MAYA FOLLOWED HER Dad's car all the way to the Headquarter's high-rise in the middle of LA. She headed into the underground, glad she'd been given a parking pass a few weeks back. She'd been here a few times to visit Claudia during her recovery. Until, of course, the day came when Claudia refused to see her. The doctors had claimed she was having difficulty coming to terms with her inability to walk. Then she'd made a sudden turnaround and was back to work as if nothing had ever happened.

Any way you looked at it, Maya had chosen to save Stefan's life. Which meant she'd also chosen to sacrifice Claudia. Although Claudia had assured her she was not upset with Maya, something told her her aunt hadn't been entirely honest. Her parents had assured Maya it would take time for Claudia to accept her new reality, and Maya had prayed she would be fine in the end.

She couldn't turn back time, but she would damn well do everything she could to make it up to her aunt.

She pulled into the parking lot beside her dad and shoved open the door to allow Sabala to get out. KALIMA had had to provide the hellhound with a special spell to allow him to enter the facility as it was standard practice to ward all agency properties against demons.

The fact that Sabala never revealed himself to anyone while within the building irked a few people. It put them on edge never knowing where the creature was, but nobody had said anything to that effect.

Maya and Sabala hurried after Dev as he headed for the elevator. Joss scrambled behind her, slipping into the elevator just in time. The small glass-walled space wasn't the best environment to be standing face-to-face with a man who was furious. The vein in his temple stood out, sharply raised.

Maya wished she'd had her mom to help defend her. She swallowed and shifted her gaze away from his.

Coward.

By the time she decided she should meet his fury head on and apologize, the elevator slid open with a woosh.

Inside the reception room they headed through the interior doors with barely a glance at its occupants. By now, the security people and the receptionist knew Maya and Joss. Joss had spent days confined to the office, manning the call-center phones during the zombie outbreak.

The girls followed Dev as he strode down the corridor, swiping his card twice before they reached the medical wing. It never failed to surprise Maya that when she stepped inside she couldn't find a difference between a proper hospital and this facility. Even this late in the day, things were humming along.

They'd spared no expense, with top-of-the-line equipment, everything in place to take care of their agents when they needed medical help. In the beginning the organization had found it difficult to explain the strange injuries received by their agents, to doctors and nurses within the public system. It hadn't taken long for them to decide that having their own medical facility made the most sense.

Sabala stopped at Maya's side as she and Joss came to a standstill while Dev spoke to a nurse in the ICU. She looked quite somber, and Dev was about to ask her something else when the doors to their right opened and Claudia rolled through in her wheelchair.

They all turned to the dark-haired woman, who despite her disability still dressed in her usual badass jeans and boots style and looked like any minute now she'd stand up and race out of the place, gun in hand, close on a demon's tail.

Claudia gave them a tight smile, the lines at the corners of her eyes pinched. "The medical team is looking at the female." She glanced at the glass doors behind him before saying. "The other one . . . is definitely dead. No doubt about it."

"How long before the autopsy is done?" Maya asked, eager to learn more about what had happened to him. The hellhound moved closer, nudging her knee as if wanting to warn her about something. She stilled the urge to scratch his head, remembering Claudia was always uncomfortable about the hellhound's invisibility.

Claude's eyebrows rose a little, but she seemed to restrain the urge to voice her thoughts. "They've already sent him down to Dr. Arturo. She will have a report sent within the hour. She's made him her priority."

Maya nodded and began to pace, leaving Sabala shifting his head left to right as he watched her.

Dev cleared his throat. "I think it's best for you and Joss to go back home. I'll bring you the report when I know something."

"I don't want to go anywhere just yet." Maya shook her head. "I want to see how she's doing."

Claudia narrowed her eyes at Maya. "Maya, are you disobeying a direct order?" Claudia's body was stiff with anger, and Maya could have sworn she'd noticed her left knee twitch. Maya glanced down at Claudia's limbs and stared, expecting the movement to repeat.

Only it didn't and when Maya lifted her gaze back to her aunt's she recognised the emotion flickering there. It lasted only a second before Claudia regained control of her features, but Maya was dead certain she'd recognise that emotion anywhere.

Fear.

What did Claudia have to be afraid of? Was it something to do with the undead, or was it more personal?

Dev frowned and held a hand up to Claudia. "Maya, that woman is dead. There's no helping her."

She stopped pacing and turned to face him, ignoring the irritation in her aunt's eyes. "So what? They'll experiment on her to find out what makes her tick?"

Dev's eyes widened, and he opened his mouth to respond. Maya lifted a hand, stopping him in mid-sentence.

"Okay. I don't believe you'd be that inhumane," she said, although she didn't miss the look Dev and Claudia exchanged. Maya inhaled. "She's sick. Dead or undead, she is aware of her surroundings, we all know most of the undead we've encountered weren't entirely aware they are gone. We all know the trouble we had rounding them up and ensuring their passing was completed."

Her dad grunted. "Yes. We all know."

Maya nodded. She hadn't forgotten her father had been in the middle of it all. Seemed at the time he was doing everything possible to stay away from the house.

Stay away from her mother.

Maya imagined it couldn't be easy for a man to discover his wife was the reincarnation of the Earth Mother. How many men could handle being married to a goddess without feeling even the slightest bit emasculated?

Add to that the fact that Leela had been forced to kill her own child. Kas was the son of the Mother Bhumi, and by virtue of that, kind of Maya's stepbrother in a weird, convoluted way.

That her mother had gone to the length of actually killing him had been as much a surprise to Maya as Dev. But then Maya's life had hung in the balance and her mother had made the best choice she could.

Claudia glided her wheelchair around so she came to a stop in front of Maya, forcing her to focus as her aunt said, "Maya, I really think you're getting ahead of yourself."

The action put Sabala on edge, and Maya had to bite her tongue as he got to his feet and placed himself between her and Claudia. Clearly the dog didn't take kindly to her aunt's tone.

"What do you mean?" asked Maya, slightly irritated.

"This is not your concern. The undead has been transferred to this facility. You've been told to go home. Our team has plenty of experience in dealing with the undead. They'll handle it from here. Your part of the mission is completed."

Maya stared at Claudia. "But-"

"No buts, Maya. As an agent you've been given an instruction and you are expected to obey it. Remain in defiance and you risk suspension."

With that, Claudia spun the wheelchair around and headed down the hall.

"What was that all about?" Maya muttered.

"She's just doing her job, Maya," said her Dad softly, although his tone was still filled with disapproval. Of Maya.

Maya sighed, and began to pace again. The doors opened and a handful of doctors flowed out. One headed for the ER and had a quiet conversation with Dev. When the doctor left, her father glanced at Maya, pausing for a moment.

He was going to tell her to wait there while he went inside, but he hesitated for a moment, as if fighting some inner war on the matter.

Then he sighed and crooked a finger in the girl's direction before turning on his heel and heading through the doors.

Despite Claudia's words, Dev was still taking her in to see the undead. Odd for him to also be defiant of the rules.

She followed him, almost trotting, knowing Joss and Sabala would be close on her heels. They headed into a small viewing room overlooking the secure hospital room. The undead female lay on the bed, skin colorless as tubes snaked around her, and her arms bore a few more IV's than Maya thought was necessary.

The hellhound took up position beside the door, as if he was making a point about not wanting to go any further into the room.

"The undead have vital signs?"

Dev laughed. "Something like that. After all the studies they did on the undead, the researchers discovered that when a person dies the body dies with them, but the brain is much slower to listen. When that person is given a second life and becomes stranded, electrical sparks begin to fire up the brain again."

"That's what makes the undead sentient even though they have no life." Joss's voice came from behind Maya. When Maya turned to look at her, her friend's gaze was focused on the body beyond the glass.

"Supremely creepy, but it totally makes sense."

She was about to ask another question when a sound came from inside the room. Sabala grunted and got to his feet, his nose pointed in the direction of the two-way window. Maya stepped closer to the glass and listened. The woman spoke and as Maya looked at her, her heart stuttered.

The zombie woman in the next room was looking straight at Maya, her eyes focused on her face. Her mouth moved and Maya strained to hear what she was saying.

The speaker on the wall was working perfectly, and Maya sucked in a breath as she heard the words.

"Tell my family."

CHAPTER 14

MAYA MET HER father's eyes, and blinked away the heat of tears. "We have to help her."

Dev gave a little shake of his head. "Best not to get emotionally involved. Especially with the undead. They're already gone. Nothing we can do to help them."

Maya glared at him, and pointed a finger at the woman in the room. "Are you telling me you're not in the least bit affected by her appeal? She's asking for her family, Dad."

"Of course, I am affected. But I'm also trying to remember she isn't alive."

"But didn't you just tell me that when an undead is resurrected, electrical impulses are activated within the person's brain."

"That's the medical description of the process."

Maya nodded. "Then wouldn't that mean memories and experiences and emotions come back to that person, even though they are not technically alive?"

Her father shrugged. "I'm not exactly clued up on the technicalities."

"But you don't have to be a rocket scientist to understand that this woman is asking for help." Maya looked at her dad. "You see her eyes? Everyone around here can tell me that she is dead, but I saw desperation in her eyes. She wants her family. She certainly doesn't want to go on a rampage killing everything in sight. What if her family have no idea she is dead? Who are we to make that decision, to decide that they don't have the right to know the truth?"

"So, what would you have us do?" he asked patiently.

"We should find them for her, Dad. No undead has ever asked for anything of us, let alone to get their family. Maybe she needs closure. I have no idea."

Joss shifted beside Maya. "I agree with Maya. We treat this woman like she means nothing, then *we* become inhuman. I know that's not what we stand for. This whole organization was created to help people. And if anyone here told me what Maya is saying is wrong, then I'm going to start questioning the integrity of the entire agency."

Maya stared, amazed at her friend's passion. Joss had always been the one ready to aid those in need. If she could have, she'd have given her trust fund over to the first person who said they needed help. Only problem with Joss was she didn't seem to have the best judgement in terms of who to help. She could all too easily be taken advantage of.

Good thing I'm here to look out for her.

Maya nodded and looked at her father. "She may have gone to the camp seeking refuge. It's obvious this isn't the kind of situation we faced when Kas let all the undead roam the Earth. Those creatures were insane with bloodlust and inhumanity. This one is . . . different. We can't just terminate her like we did back then. Her fingerprints should tell us who she is. With that we can find her family."

Her father sighed. "You have a unique way of thinking. And you have a true heart. The older you grow, the more I see similarities between you and The Mother."

It had taken a while for Maya to accept her origins. When her parents had first explained it to her, she'd found it completely unbelievable. But the dreams she'd had, had allowed her to see the truth.

Maya was the reincarnation of a holy priestess, the teacher who'd spearheaded the organization for which her parents worked. She was also the woman who'd taken her mother, an abused wife, under her wing and turned her from a submissive girl into a strong woman.

From her own ragged memories, Maya knew the Mother had been frustrated with her job. Despite her caring and benevolent ways, the mother had had a passionate streak within her and on her deathbed she'd begged the goddess Kali for an opportunity to help her in a more physical way.

The goddess had given her the boon she'd requested, allowing the Mother to be born again. As Maya. For a long time, Maya had hated the idea that she wasn't her own person. It had taken weeks for her to reconcile the reality of her life now, with the powers Kali had given her, and the life she'd lived in her past to earn it.

Although she didn't retain all the memories from her previous life, Maya did remember enough to understand it was the real thing, not another figment of her parent's imagination.

Maya nodded and gave her father a gentle smile. "I'm beginning to see the same thing myself."

He raised his eyebrows and turned to her, completely forgetting the problem at hand. "You're remembering your past life as the Mother?"

Maya shook her head. Even though she'd remembered a few things, she wasn't ready to admit it to her parents. She'd seen the utter devotion the two of them had had for the Mother, and it made her uncomfortable when they looked at her with that same expression.

Weird.

She shook her head again. "No. Nothing specific. Just feelings."

Dev looked disappointed, but he gave her an encouraging smile before looking out into the room. The woman was sleeping now, although her face did not look in the least bit peaceful.

Machines beeped, and her chest rose and fell.

Dev nodded. "Okay. We'll start with her identity, and go from there. I'll keep you posted."

Maya smiled. Her instinct had been to reach out and give him a hug, to show her gratitude.

Was she now too old for simple things like hugs? Was there some kind of separation between her and her parents, now that her memories of her previous life were returning? Maya hoped it didn't mean she was going to end up turning into the Mother and losing everything she'd been as Maya.

Her head was beginning to hurt, all the thoughts convoluted, the haunting echo of drums in a distant part of her mind. A cool wet nose pressed against the palm of her hand and Maya blinked the haze away, never more grateful for Sabala than at that moment.

Unaware of Maya's distress, Dev turned to leave. The girls and the dog followed him out of the room. Her dad paused only long enough to give them instructions to return home and to assure Maya that they still needed to talk. Then he headed to the elevator, mumbling something about fingerprint analysis.

Maya wasn't too worried. She'd done what she'd done for the right reasons. They just needed to see it for themselves, and Maya was pretty sure they soon would. She'd done the right thing. Surely they won't be blind to it?

Of course, Claudia may well be another story altogether. Maya didn't want to think about her aunt's anger, or the strange emotions she'd seen on her face.

She refocused on her dad and was relieved he was doing as she asked. For a moment there she'd thought he was going to say no. The trio headed for the car, Maya driving them home in a comfortable silence with Sabala sitting quietly on the back seat.

At last, Joss broke the silence as she cleared her throat. "So what do you think Nik would think of this whole debacle?"

Maya glanced at her briefly before turning her attention to the asphalt. She shrugged. "He shouldn't be against it. He has a whole army of demons at his beck and call. Surely he understands that if demons are sentient then undead could be too?"

Joss was silent, giving Maya an uncertain glance.

Maya sighed. "Even if he doesn't agree with my actions, he should be able to tell us if sentience if even possible in the undead."

Joss still looking uncertain. Then she cleared her throat. "Have you heard anything from Ria?"

Maya nodded. "Mom said she's settled. Her surgery has been completed."

"When do we get to see her?" asked Joss eagerly.

Maya shrugged. "Mom says she needs to come to terms with her new self. If she wants to have a life in which she interacts with us again, her new persona has to be foolproof."

Joss made a face.

Maya understood exactly how she felt. It had been so hard for them to see Ria leave. Their friend had been in a dangerous situation. Her fiancé, like Leela's first spouse, had beaten her within an inch of her life. Fortunately Ria had confessed to Maya, and Maya had brought her mom in to help.

Best thing she could ever have done for her friend.

Ria had been taken under the wing of KALIMA, given a new identity, and now a new face. She'd requested to be placed somewhere where she would still be able to see Maya and Joss.

What had surprised Maya was Ria's admission that she wanted to be actively involved in KALIMA too. Ria had always been the quiet one, so reserved, so accepting of male domination. Maya would never have imagined her friend as a bad-ass zombie killer. But, that's exactly what Ria wanted to be. And from what Maya had heard, nothing was going to stop her.

Suppose being married to an unmentionable-profane-word-for-a-male-body-part would do it for any girl.

Maya was so proud of her friend that she could cry. "I just can't wait to see her again"

Joss nodded. "You and me both, sister."

Maya grinned as she turned into the drive.

"Yes. You and me both, sister."

CHAPTER 15

MAYA AND JOSS returned home, a little drained from the excitement of the evening.

They were walking into the kitchen when Maya's mom entered on their heels. Clearly she'd been waiting for them to return. Probably working in the living room, lying in wait.

"Don't you ever listen?" asked Leela, anger making her voice vibrate. Sabala, standing just inside the kitchen door, chose that moment to let out a soft whuff, as if in warning.

A little late, pooch.

Maya shook her head, knowing exactly what her mom meant. "I know what you're going to say, Mom. But I had to go."

"I don't think you understand that sometimes there are consequences to your actions." Leela was staring at her, spine stiff, stance saying she wasn't about to back down.

Maya frowned. She opened her mouth, intent on asking what her mom meant when Leela waved a hand at her daughter and cut her off. "You have to think of the big picture. And you have to pick your battles. You were injured, Maya. This time you were lucky. One dead and one too sick to be a danger. But what if either or both had been dangerous? And you'd gone out there without having healed sufficiently, you would have been more of a danger to your father and Joss then you would have been any help."

Maya suppressed a sigh. She deserved the telling off. Already had one from Claudia in the last hour. An encounter that had left Maya with more than just the feeling of regret. Something was up with Claude. Maybe she deserved her aunt's anger.

But only she knew how well she'd felt. It wasn't as if she was an invalid, but she had to accept that her mom was worried.

"But I was helpful. If I hadn't been there, neither one of them would have found the zombie. Or rather, *both* the zombies." Maya paused, feeling a little vindicated.

Leela let out a heated breath. Despite her cream silk pajamas and her dark hair draped over her shoulders, she looked like a dangerous woman. "You totally didn't get what I was trying to say, did you?"

But Maya nodded quickly. "I did get what you were trying to say. But I just can't sit by and watch everyone else try to do something I can do so easily. It took me less than ten minutes to complete the job."

Joss grunted beside her, and Maya turned to look at her friend. She was glaring at Maya, an angry look on her face.

Shaking her head, Maya said, "I know what you're thinking. And, no, I don't think you're less capable. I just think that with the powers I've been given, things are much easier for me. And I think it makes a ton more sense if I'm allowed to do those things. It only helps the rest of the team."

"And how do you think being injured helps the team?" asked Leela.

Maya glanced at her mom, her face still red with anger.

"But I'm fine now."

Leela's eyebrow curved. "But that's not the point. This time you're fine. But will you make the right decision the next time?" She sighed. "What if in the future, you're injured so badly you can barely move? Will your stubbornness allow you to accept you're injured and need time to heal, or will you do what you did today and race out of the house to do something that could easily have been done by somebody else, and probably injure yourself more in the process?"

Maya rolled her eyes. "Don't you think you're being a little bit dramatic?"

Leela stopped in her tracks, turned to meet her daughter's eyes, and placed her hands on her hips.

Her eyes burned with fury.

"I don't think you understand the big picture." Leela shook her head, her expression one of fear. "It's all well and good for you to go off half-cocked, but nobody ever wins a war just because they were lucky enough to win a skirmish. You should have been more concerned about your own health, considering *you* may one day be responsible for saving us all."

"Now, you're really being dramatic." Maya fidgeted, then folded her arms as she glanced over at Sabala whose ears had lifted at her tone.

"She's not being dramatic," said Joss. "Your mom is only saying that everyone around here is worried about you. And yes we are a little bit selfish in our concern. We can help ourselves now, but not too long ago *you* were the one who saved us all. And we all understand that there may come a day in the future, where *you* will be called upon to save us again. If you behave recklessly and endanger your life in the meantime, *you* are in effect endangering our own future."

Leela took a step closer. She put a hand on Maya's shoulder. "Not to mention the fact that while you may have Kali's powers, you are not immortal. You can die."

Maya stiffened beneath Leela's touch. She forced her feet to move. Shrugging off her mom's hand, she rounded the wooden table and went to the other side of the kitchen. The whole conversation was suffocating her and she needed space, needed to put the table between herself and her mother and friend.

They may be right, but she didn't want to admit it.

Not right now.

Her mind went back to a few weeks ago when she'd had to fight for her life, for their lives. When things had gone so crazy that the dead were walking the streets, unable to pass on to the underworld because Lord Yama was powerless to do his job since he'd been locked up by a crazy demon king. Then, Maya had been called upon to use all the powers given to her by the goddess Kali.

To save the world.

She'd never wanted such a responsibility. And yet, she had little choice in the matter. People relied on her whether she wanted them to or not.

Hadn't she asked for this life when she'd died in her previous one?

She wanted to shake the thoughts off. Could Maya, in her new reincarnation, really be responsible for what her previous self had wanted? Was it fair to expect her to live her entire life as one person only to discover she wasn't who she thought she was?

She'd accepted it, though.

Both her past life and the powers Kali had given her. She'd moved on from denial and helplessness, to acceptance. And she'd trained and dedicated herself to the efforts of KALIMA.

Figured she'd need to work through a few more of her issues before she could even hope to attain some measure of peace.

"Fine." Her voice held a defiant note to it, but her family was right. "I'll admit you *may* have a point. But that doesn't mean I have to sit back and relax and watch while you all go off and fight demons and the creepy bad guys."

Joss laughed. "You know that's not what we're trying to say. I think you're just being stupid now."

Maya glared at her, but Joss was right. She was just angry, and being defensive. She was being childish. Wasn't it time she began to act like an adult?

Maya straightened her spine and opened her mouth to respond.

She didn't get the opportunity.

The air beside her mom shivered as Nik solidified.

Maya's heart thumped the way it always did when her boyfriend appeared.

About time, demigod.

<h1 style="text-align:center">CHAPTER 16</h1>

OSS LEANED AGAINST the table as Nik arrived. She cocked her head at the demigod and gave him a cool smile. "Hopefully you're here to back us up," she said dryly.

He smiled as he reached out to scratch Sabala on the head. He and Joss had a comfortable camaraderie and he'd read her subtle nuances almost from their first meeting. Now, he didn't take her attitude to heart. "What's going on?" he asked, his curious gaze going from Joss, to Maya and then to her mom.

Leela surged into action, headed for the cupboard beside the stove, and began to pull out pots and spoons. Without turning, she said, "It's time you spoke to Maya about running recklessly into situations without backup." She slammed the pot onto the stove and Maya flinched as the sound clanged around the kitchen.

Her mom was pulling condiments out of a nearby cupboard and Maya wanted to smile. Leela liked to cook when she was frustrated. Or angry. There were a few times Maya recalled walking into the kitchen to find cakes, cookies, dinner and fresh bread filling the air with deliciousness. That usually happened on the back end of an argument with Maya's dad.

Apparently there was something about the process that calmed her down.

Nik gave Leela a quizzical look, then turned his attention to Maya. "What did you do?"

Maya glared at him. "You're taking their side?"

He lifted a shoulder. "I'm not exactly sure what happened, but if they're pissed off with you, you probably deserve it."

"*You* are a lot of help." She wanted to be angry with him for not backing her up, but deep down she knew he was unshakeable in his morals. Which meant he'd take the right side even if it meant being in opposition to Maya.

Now, Mr Too-good-to-be-true sighed as if the weight of the world lay upon his shoulders. "We're only here to help you. I'm assuming your mom and Joss are merely worried about you."

"Worried about me as if I am a five-year-old," Maya snapped, adding Nik to the list of people already annoyed with her.

Leela tugged the fridge open really hard. "That's not it, and you know it."

Maya did know it. And she felt ashamed. She kept fighting this battle, even though she knew her mom was right. One day her pride was going to be her downfall.

She sighed and said nothing, turning her gaze back to Nik who was now watching her thoughtfully. He looked tired, and annoyed.

Great.

He was angry with her.

Maya took a deep breath, trying to calm herself. No sense in allocating blame to the people around her when she was as much to blame, if not completely. As if sensing her frustration Sabala left his post and rounded the table, his claws clicking against the tiles. He stopped beside her and sat back on his haunches, leaving her to wonder if he was there to protect her, or to protect her family from her.

"I understand everyone's concern. I really do." She glanced at her mom who looked far from convinced. "I do Mom, I really do. The only reason I went out was because I'd been able to heal my feet. You know I can heal my body using my fire. You should also know I wouldn't do anything reckless. I healed myself enough to be able to defend myself if necessary."

Despite her defense, she'd been reckless. All she'd done was a cursory healing, and she understood now she should have done more. Especially since she ended up having to heal herself while she was beneath the bridge. If she'd had a little more patience, she'd have been in much better condition.

She schooled her features. "So, as you can see, I wasn't being reckless. I was fine. Fine enough to drive all the way there, and to find two undead where Dad and Joss only knew to look for one. We all know my nose works better than anyone else's around here. That is what found the second zombie. My ability to smell."

Nobody responded.

"And right now the woman is lying at the HQ facility, safe from harming others and from being harmed herself." Maya was forced to fill the silence.

She turned to Nik and raised an eyebrow. "I'm assuming you have some news for us. I hardly think you came back so you could join them in scolding me."

His lips did that funny twist telling Maya he was trying to stop himself from smiling.

Despite the fact that he'd sided with her mom and Joss, Maya understood he cared about her. She could be defensive at any other time. Right now, she was too tired to bother.

Nik nodded.

"I have news, and it's not good."

Maya felt her heart tighten.

Nik cleared his throat. "We have received numerous reports

of dancers who died of exhaustion and dehydration over the last month."

Maya sighed.

A deep sadness filled her. The dream she'd had was more than just a dream.

She waited for Nik, who seemed to be contemplating the best way to reveal his news.

"There were three cases this week that we know of. One in Germany, and two in India."

"Any other similarities besides dehydration and exhaustion?" asked Maya taking a step forward to grasp the edge of the table.

Her hands had begun to shake, and she wanted to do something with them because she knew any physical sign of fear would be detrimental to her position within her team. She had to always ensure she put on a strong face. She couldn't afford to have her family doubt her confidence.

Nik nodded. "Yes, bloody feet were also a common factor. One of the dancers had participated in a dance competition in India. Indian classical dance," he replied. "That's Germany. Of the two in India, one is Kathak, and the other one was Bharatanayam. So both North and South Indian classical forms.

Joss clicked her tongue. "When was the last time we had a spate of deaths with the victims being exclusively dancers?"

Nik glanced at her. "It's definitely not a coincidence. Don't worry, we find this too much of a concern to let it lie. The German victim was found dead on the stage after her performance."

Maya took the stool nearest to her, sinking onto it slowly. She rubbed her forehead and stared at Nik, the sound of drums and bells reverberating in her head. Before she knew what she was doing, she'd fisted both her hands and stiffened her spine with all her might so her body wouldn't go nuts and throw itself into dance.

"Maya," asked her mom. "You okay."

Maya sighed, feeling her heart thumping hard against her ribs. "I'm not exactly sure how I feel." She looked up at her mom. "How are you supposed to feel when you realize the dream you had could possibly be your own vision of the last moments of an innocent girl's life?"

She swallowed hard and watched the darkness fill her mother's eyes. She knew Leela, even being the reincarnation of a goddess, suffered deeply for everything Maya went through. It was one of the reasons Maya never dismissed her mother's opinion or feeling.

And right now, she watched her mom hurt for her and all she wanted to do was to erase that pain.

CHAPTER 17

After a restless night's sleep, in which Maya was thankfully not plagued with dreams of bloody feet and entrancing music, she spent a quiet morning practicing with her fire, with Joss spotting for her.

After lunch the girls went back to the mundane, schoolwork that wouldn't get done and submitted if they didn't actually complete and submit it. Maya spent a couple hours working through a Calculus assignment. The numbers kept her mind focused on something other than dead girls.

When Nik knocked on her bedroom door she almost jumped off her chair.

She glared at him but her awareness of the concern in his expression made Maya forget her annoyance.

Nik cleared his throat. "We need to get going."

"Where to?" she asked. She got to her feet, curious now, her work forgotten.

Nik said, "To check out a new crime scene before it's contaminated."

"It's recent?" Her heart began to race.

Nik shifted on his feet and said, "Yes. Very recent."

Nik transported Maya to the Apollo Theatre in London's West End.

"I'm sure I'm supposed to be excited I'm finally here, but the circumstances of this visit kills it all."

Maya stared out from the stage at the multitude of red seats curving along the room in an elegant semicircle. The gold-toned balconies and wall decor seemed garish in the bright lights, but Maya suspected it was more the reason she was here that sullied the drama and majesty of the famous theatre.

"We should be alone for a while, but just in case, I've erected a protective circle around the stage. Local law enforcement are here in full force. We can study the body and the scene without being disturbed, but we have to be quick."

Maya nodded, knowing Nik's protective magic would make anyone approaching forget why they were there in the first place. That wouldn't last for too long considering higher ups would be looking for answers and people would get suspicious sooner or later.

Better make this quick.

Maya walked around Nik and came to a sudden halt. The floor before her was awash with streaks of blood. To an untrained eye, that's all they would be; blood smears.

But Maya studied the lines, and as she followed them, images flitted through her mind, as if she could see what was happening with her own two eyes. Though unfamiliar with classical dance, she was able to identify a pattern. From her experience with the dream not too long ago, she saw the movements of the girl's feet that had created the bloody prints.

She pointed at the smooth, neater streaks. "Here. See these marks. How much cleaner they are than the rest?" Nik nodded. "I think this was when she began to lose control. Maybe she'd grown tired? But from there on, you can tell how the smears become messy and uneven. Almost random."

"The police reported inexplicable blood trails. Apparently they were unable to identify them."

Maya nodded. "I only recognize them because I had that dream." Maya paused. "Well, not a dream any longer. Although, to be honest, I'd prefer if it was just my imagination."

Nik glanced over Maya's shoulder and she knew immediately what he was looking at. From the moment they'd arrived, she'd tried not to look at it. She'd even studied the patterns of blood smears to avoid the sheet-covered body sprawled to the right of the stage.

Now she had no choice.

Nik moved past her and Maya turned on her heel really slowly. She took a breath and held it as she followed him to the body. They kept to the side of the bloody floor so as not to create more footprints.

"The blood is still wet," Maya said softly as they drew closer to the dead girl.

"Death is estimated as at forty minutes ago."

Maya looked up at Nik's face, his features hooded as he stared down at the covered corpse. He crouched down and took hold of the edge of the sheet, drawing it away from the girl's face.

Maya silenced a gasp. The girl's skin was alabaster pale even though Maya could tell that she was of a duskier complexion. She wore a complicated outfit made from deep blue and red silk shot with gold thread. Gathers and pleats, tapered pants and delicate blouse. Her skin appeared gray and bloodless, and her makeup made her look like a mannequin.

"What was she doing here so late?"

"Her parents obtained permission for her to practice before her performance tomorrow. She's always been dedicated. Practices two hours every morning before she heads to school. This exam performance was a culmination of four years of study."

Maya swallowed hard. It was such a waste. Of the girl's effort. Of her talent. Maya forced herself to remain emotionless. She had to be objective. So she studied the body.

Dancers applied their makeup with a heavier hand to allow the full effect to be seen from the audience. Close up, a glance at any dancer's face would be disconcerting, but watching the performance from the audience, most people would never guess.

Now, the thick layer of makeup made it harder to identify the girl's expression, but Maya had known the moment she saw her face that she'd been terrified at the moment of her death.

"She was scared," Maya whispered, sinking down beside Nik.

He glanced at her, curious.

"Her face. She looks terrified," Maya said, almost choking as memories flooded back to her. "I know exactly what she felt."

Nik curled an arm around her shoulders but the rush of emotions was too much and she flinched. He seemed to understand because he removed his arm and rubbed her back slowly, just a gentle touch to say he was there for her, but that he wouldn't overwhelm her.

He bent close to her ear. "What do you think happened?"

Maya inhaled slowly, then pulled the sheet away from the girl's feet. They were swollen, and bruised, covered in cuts and clotted blood.

She pointed to the girl's feet. "She wouldn't have felt that until the end."

Maya shifted her gaze to the girl's face.

"She would have come out, played the music, then began to dance. A few minutes in she would have felt a strange pull of energy, and then the dance would have increased in speed. A good time later she'd have struggled, perspiring, fatigued, breathless. And in a lot of pain. She would have become aware of the trance taking control over her. Or at least I think she would have. I guess it depends on whether she was sensitive to the trance in the first place."

Nik nodded. "Many people are not susceptible to the trance. Some say that it is only the holier, more spiritual people that feel the pull of it."

"But we both know that's BS."

Nik gave a subdued smile, aware, like Maya, that this wasn't the place to joke around.

Focusing on the girl, Maya said, "She may have struggled when she felt her feet hurt. I think that would have been painful enough to cut through whatever was controlling her."

"So the perspiration resulted in dehydration."

Maya nodded.

"But that means she'd have been dancing for hours."

"Yeah. A lot of hours. Which explains the damaged feet."

"How long? Can you hazard a guess?"

Shrugging, Maya said, "I'm not sure. An autopsy would help clarify that." Maya met Nik's gaze. "Can we get access to the results?"

Nik looked at the dead girl. "We'll put out feelers, and see where we get. I have someone in MI5."

"You have someone everywhere," said Maya dryly.

As Maya got to her feet, her mind filled with the beat of drums and the melody of a violin. A wave of dizziness washed over her and she threw out her hands as she felt her body fall. She felt Nik grab hold of her arm.

And found herself kneeling beside the girl, her fingers immersed in the pool of blood surrounding the body, with Nik leaning close. "What happened?" he asked, shock clear in his eyes.

Maya shook her head. "I don't know. It felt like some kind of energy pulling on my mind." Maya gasped and stared at Nik. "It was exactly the same thing I felt in the dream.

They both looked at the girl, lying there prone and lifeless.

"You said you felt a strange energy while dancing, and then now again, a wave of energy."

Maya nodded.

"And dancing creates emotional and spiritual energy.

"Does it also create cosmic energy?" asked Maya softly as she got to her feet and wiped her fingers off on her jeans.

Nik didn't answer. He just stared at the girl. "Cosmic energy is a precious commodity."

Maya's eyes widened. "Someone is sucking the energy out of the dancers to collect cosmic energy."

Things just keep getting better and better.

CHAPTER 18

MAYA AND NIK arrived back at the house, both sunk deep within their own thoughts. They entered the kitchen to find a pot of chicken curry simmering on low and the table half set with plates and spoons but no glasses or placemats.

Maya frowned at the state of abandonment, and gave Nik a confused glance. Even Sabala was missing from the scene.

A handbag sat beside the kitchen table, which gave Maya a reason to smile. There was only one person she knew who carried a bright pink alligator purse.

Claudia.

Was she here to reprimand her some more? Or was it time for Maya to face the music and maybe get suspended or something.

Hope not.

They'd be overreacting especially since so much good had come from her actions. Why would they make such a big deal out of it?

Maya turned on her heel and hurried out of the kitchen down the passage, keeping an ear out for voices. As expected, she found her visitor in the study with her parents. Joss, though, seemed to be missing. Probably preoccupied or studying.

Joss had seemed distracted after her visit with a parents. Maya made a mental note to make some time to talk to Joss because she knew her friend would need it.

From the door, Maya studied the trio in the study. They looked like a group of friends gathered to chat about nothing. But Maya wondered when the last time was they'd discussed a movie or a concert, or something equally innocuous. Chances were, this visit would be more about demons and demonic possession.

Maya entered the room, a bright smile on her face. The smile was her only defense against the tightening in her heart. She knew full well Claudia had been pretty mad with her.

Now she tried hard to keep her eyes off the wheelchair in which Claudia sat. Three heads turned as Maya moved into the room.

"Hey, honey," said her mom with a smile. A smile that held a slight edge of concern which was amplified by the fact that her mom was stroking Sabala's dark head.

Maya smiled and hurried to Claudia's side. "Hey you," she said reaching out to give Claudia a hug that could be had in the privacy of their home. At the agency everyone behaved totally professional, no hugs or personal references. And Claudia was the strictest about it.

In the past, hugs had always been something they'd enjoyed, like two girlfriends meeting after a long time. Although Claudia had been her mother's friend, she had also been Maya's own confidant.

Though Maya felt Claudia's arms gather her close, she sensed something was missing. She ignored the little hollow in her heart and gave her aunt a squeeze.

As Maya released her and got back to her feet, Claudia said, "Where have you been?"

Maya sighed and sank into the seat opposite her aunt. She sensed Nik walk into the room but he remained just inside the doorway.

Her dad gave him a nod, and her mom, who was leaning against the side of the desk, smiled at him. He was comfortable with them now, not needing to give anyone formal greetings. Which was a relief.

Claudia twisted in her wheelchair, her black hair gleaming as she moved. She smiled up at Nik. "Well, look what the cat dragged in. How are you, Nik?" Her smile was bright and friendly, and she looked gorgeous, Maya had to admit.

"They keep me busy. And by *they* I mean everyone on top of the world as well as under it." Nik smiled, and Claudia gave a soft laugh.

Then she turned to Maya. "So . . . do tell." Her tone and demeanor was much more relaxed now and she almost seemed like a different person to the woman who'd chewed Maya out yesterday.

Maya nodded. "The girl at the theatre in London was killed in much the same way as I'd dreamed."

"She danced herself to her death?"

Maya nodded. "Yes, she showed all the signs I'd experienced in the dream. Perspiration, and dehydration, and of course bloody, broken feet. The skin had been damaged in the same way as mine had, only much worse."

"So whatever you experienced in your dream was multiplied in reality?"

Maya sighed. "She's been forced to dance, controlled by some awful power, she looked like she'd perspired until her entire body was dehydrated. Also, her feet looked like they had been beaten to a pulp. There was blood everywhere . . . the entire stage was covered in it."

Maya's voice broke as she looked down at her hands, at her blood-stained fingers. She was unable to continue talking about what she'd seen, unable to handle recalling the dream and under-standing entirely what the girl been going through. She shook her head. Then swallowed hard, and slipped her hands inside her pockets hoping nobody had seen the proof of the horror she'd witnessed.

Claudia tilted her head, her dark eyes shining with compassion. She held out her hands and Maya automatically reached out for them. She took Maya's hand in hers, holding them in her lap squeezing it lightly. "I'm so sorry you had to go through that. I can see it's been hard on you."

Maya nodded, the movement jerky as Claudia's thigh muscles shifted beneath her hand. She stiffened. But that wasn't possible. It was just Maya's imagination gone crazy.

She sniffed and said, "It's just the dream was so intense, and so painful. And when I saw the girl lying there dead on the stage, it was as if I knew exactly what she'd been through, pain and terror . . . and everything."

Claudia squeezed her hand. "I know honey, consider yourself fortunate that all you experienced was the dream and not the reality."

Maya's heart tightened, she could have sworn she'd heard an odd edge to Claudia's voice. A hint of hardness that made Maya wonder what Claudia was really saying.

As she gave Claudia a bright smile, Sabala trotted over and took up post beside her. She glanced at the hellhound and wondered what he'd sensed for him to leave her mom and come to her. Had he also felt something off about Claudia?

Maya said, "I'll be fine. And you're right. For me it was just a dream, and I appreciate that. Especially now, having seen the reality. It's a horrible way to die." Maya took a deep breath, turning her attention to her parents. "We need to find her killer. Nik has a theory."

She glanced over her shoulder at Nik, who took a few steps closer to the desk. He leaned against the bookshelf at his back and said, "We know the energy a dancer creates is powerful. And we know the more talented the dancer, the more energy she creates. We're just wondering if that's why only the most talented dancers were targeted."

Claudia frowned. "So you suspect the killer is after the energy the girls created?" Her tone hardened and Maya noticed her skin go a little pale. This whole thing seemed to be affecting everyone on a deeper level. Maya just hoped it would be over fast before it took a greater toll on them all.

Nik nodded. "Exactly that. I'm going to start putting feelers out, find any possible suspects with a history of hoarding or abusing cosmic energy."

Dev nodded. "And I'll do the same with KALIMA."

There was a moment of silence, in which Dev turned his attention to Claudia. He gave a short nod, and said, "You can fill us in now."

Claudia smiled, and Maya could have sworn it had a tight edge to it. She blinked, trying to ease her mind as to her suspicion.

Claudia shifted her gaze, meeting Maya's eyes. "I have news regarding the undead woman you found. We ran her fingerprints and identified her. And we found her family."

Maya leaned forward. "Who was she?"

With a slight shake of the head, Claudia gave Maya's dad a glance. It was as if she wanted permission to continue, reminding Maya of Dev's seniority.

He gave the nod and Claudia said, "Carly Matthews. From Santa Monica. She had one child - a girl. Her parents thought she'd run away. They came over and identified the body."

Maya stiffened.

"The body?"

CHAPTER 19

"**Y**ES," SAID CLAUDIA. She seemed to be watching Maya carefully. "A priest had been called in to perform the ritual. From previous experience we know the undead rarely survive final rites."

Dev laughed. "It's not as if we want them to survive."

Maya glared at her dad. "Why wouldn't we?"

"Maya, they need to move on to the next plane. We can't have undead walking around as if they belong on earth."

Maya shook her head. "You didn't see what I saw. She was sentient. She was aware. It wasn't as if she was some kind of crazed zombie. You saw it. She asked for help."

Dev shifted forward and settled his elbows on the table "Maya, surely you can't seriously be suggesting we allow them to live. So to speak."

Maya nodded. "Why not? Who are we to say who lives or dies?" Maya's thoughts were for the woman's child more than anything.

"Why are you thinking this way all of a sudden?" asked Leela. She looked concerned. As if she thought Maya had lost all her marbles.

"Because until now, I'd never come face-to-face with one. Has anyone ever taken the time to sit and have a conversation with one of them? Yes, I know they died. Their lives have been expunged. And they did come back to life in a body that was technically dead. I understand all of that. But if their minds are still conscious, how can we say we are in the right by killing them. They're still people. If she asked for her family then doesn't it mean the undead still know who they are, and they still know their families? Not all these people had risen from the grave. So many of them died without their families knowing. Don't you think it's our duty to help reunite them with their families?"

Claudia laughed. "Come on, Maya. This is bordering on the ridiculous. Our job is to make sure they complete the journey to Patala. What do you think Yama would think of this new plan of yours?"

There was a hard note to her voice. She seemed angry, her tone filled with derision. Maya glanced at her mum, a question in her eyes. Leela was frowning, the glance she gave Claudia questioning her attitude.

Maya wasn't sure whether she should be relieved. She'd never foreseen a time when the relationship between her family and Claudia would be threatened. She wasn't about to push the issue now. If her mom was becoming aware of the tension that was all that was needed.

Nik cleared his throat. "I'd be happy to take the proposition to Yama. I'm sure he would take it into consideration."

Claudia laughed again, this time coldly. "You think Yama would consider keeping zombies alive?"

Nik tilted his head, studying Claudia. "All I'm saying is he would *consider* the option. He may not agree. Or, he may agree to allow them a short space of time in which to say goodbye." He glanced at Maya, his expression softening. "I think that's all Maya wants. I highly doubt she's expecting us to leave the undead walking around without ever reaching the gates of Patala."

Maya smiled, relieved he understood. "It's exactly what I was trying to say. Of course, I wouldn't expect them to remain on earth forever."

Claudia sighed and sat back. "Thank goodness. For a moment there I thought you were going off your head." Maya wasn't sure what to say to that so she said nothing. Claudia inhaled. "I've been a bit worried about you, Maya."

"Worried?" asked Maya, frowning.

Claudia nodded. "Yes. You displayed an amazing amount of carelessness in the Waterfront case. Your rash behavior has a few people shaking their heads. It also has people more concerned than ever."

"More concerned about what?"

"People are beginning to wonder how safe you are. You behaving rashly, without thinking, and acting even in spite of advice to the contrary."

Maya was stunned at Claudia's sudden attack. She could hear the hardness in her aunt's tone, and she felt the corresponding hurt bloom within her.

"But I've explained that my actions were not rash. I'm fully capable of healing myself. I knew what I was doing when I left the house. And if I hadn't been there we wouldn't have found both undead."

Maya was repeating herself, but she said it anyway. As she fell silent, she glanced at her parent's faces. The expressions were confused. As if Claudia had not discussed this with them first. What was Claudia up to?

Even Sabala seemed concerned as he placed his head on Maya's lap and stared across at Claudia. Nik, though, was oddly silent and Maya refused to turn and look at him. What if he too was critical of her decision? This whole thing was getting way out of hand.

Claudia huffed, giving the dog a dark look. "You always have an explanation for everything, don't you?" She shifted forward on her chair and glared at Maya. "Just for your information, there are consequences for your actions."

She didn't have to point at her useless legs. Maya's eyes fell on them of their own accord. She was dealing with her guilt about what had happened to Claudia. And it seemed Claudia was dealing with her anger at Maya.

Months had gone by where Claudia had smiled and pretended everything was all right. That she was adjusting to her new life based at headquarters and coordinating a team from a distance. Claudia seemed to be quite good at it. Yet clearly she had been harboring this rage.

"I know there are consequences," Maya said softly, staring at Claudia's legs.

When she glanced up at Claudia's face, she knew her aunt had seen the focus of her gaze. And from her expression Maya got the impression she wanted her to feel guilty.

Mission accomplished.

"I'm sorry. And I don't think I will ever stop being sorry for what happened to you."

Claudia shook her head, her eyes dark. "This is nothing to do with me."

Although words said one thing, her eyes and her expressions said something else. Maya knew, and accepted, that Claudia wasn't ready to admit she was angry with her. She was ready to take out her anger on Maya in an indirect way, though.

Maya wasn't sure how to handle that.

She sat back as Claudia said, "It has to do with how you function as part of the team. No matter who you are, no matter what powers you have, you have to be part of that cohesive unit. Which means working together. That is what concerns us. From past experience we've seen you tend to have a reactionary method, which means you don't wait for a plan to be created. You just let your gut tell you what to do, and you go out and do it."

Claudia was right, but being put on the spot also put Maya on the defensive. Maya shook her head. "You know as well as I do that that's not the case."

Claudia lifted a hand, the movement silencing Maya in an instant. "This is not up for discussion, Maya. Consider yourself warned. There are many people within the organization who are concerned there may be more consequences in the future for the agents who work with you."

Maya jostled Sabala as she got to her feet. She didn't bother looking at her parents or Nik for their support. "If you're so worried about the team, then why don't you just let me work on my own?"

Claudia shook her head. "Because that's not how we work. That may be how *you* want to work. But at KALIMA that's not how we run our agency. You need to rethink your position if that's what you want."

Maya tried to control the anger growing within her. What was it Claudia was trying to do? To Maya it felt as if she was trying to push her out of the agency.

Why would Claudia want to do that?

"What's going on? Why are you doing this? The powers Kali has given me only ever helped us. Why would you prefer the agency not have the benefit of Kali's powers?"

"Just because you have the power, doesn't mean you are any better than us at our jobs."

"Claudia," said Dev, frowning as he stared at her. "What's going on? Where's this coming from?"

Claudia tilted her head, lifting her chin as she stared at him, an iciness in her eyes that had never been there before. "Sorry to have to tell you this, but *your* position has also been compromised."

"Compromised how?" Dev said, his eyes tightening with anger.

Maya had never seen such an expression on his face when speaking to Claudia. If anything they'd all had an immense love and respect for her. Maya wanted to cry as the realization hit her that their relationship with Claudia may just be over.

Claudia grabbed hold of the wheels of her wheelchair and pushed it forward so she came abreast of the desk, her sudden movement sending Sabala straight to his feet and on guard. Maya patted him on his head and he sank back onto his haunches although his attention didn't move from her aunt.

She allowed herself to look over at Nik. Bet Nik hadn't known what he was in for when he dropped by to report his findings. His expression was dark and he looked confused and frustrated. So he too was wondering what was wrong with Claudia.

Claudia remained oblivious of the hellhound's concern. "This has been discussed in your absence because we know you'll be biased. With Maya being your daughter, you're immediately prejudiced in this argument."

"What argument?" asked Leela, the hurt in her eyes clear as she studied her friend's face.

"The one in which Maya is a danger to us all."

CHAPTER 20

CLAUDIA SHIFTED HER gaze, staring at her friend now, defiance in her eyes.

"Maya is a danger to us?" said Leela, her tone hardening as her eyes narrowed. Maya could see she was priming for a fight.

Claudia nodded, seemingly oblivious to the danger. It wasn't a secret that Leela now possessed powers, powers given to her from the mother goddess Bhumi. Maybe not as powerful as the ones Maya received from Kali, but Leela was not incapable of killing Claudia.

Maybe Claudia didn't notice.

Probably for the best.

Maya glanced at her mom, raising her eyebrows in an attempt to get her to calm down. But it seemed Leela couldn't be swayed. She turned her attention back to Claudia, waiting for her response.

"Isn't it obvious she is a danger? Everything she's done these last few weeks shows she's dangerous. And I'm not even talking about what happened to me."

"You can't talk about what happened to you. Because you and I both know that those were choices Maya had to make to save

Stefan's life. At the time, you said you would have done the same thing. To be quite honest, if I'd been in Maya's position, I would have as well. It wasn't a decision made because Maya had powers. It was a decision made with the life of a person in mind."

Claudia shook her head. "This is not about me. I stand by what I said at the time. I probably would have done the same thing myself."

Claudia was saying the words, but Maya could see they were a lie. A glance at Leela confirmed she too knew her friend was lying. It was a lot for Maya to accept.

She wanted to burst into tears. She was watching the death off her mom's friendship with Claudia. The death of the sister-hood that had lasted more than two decades. She could tell how deeply hurt her mother was, and there was nothing Maya could do about it.

Leela cleared her throat and Sabala shifted his gaze to watch Maya's mom. The hellhound knew exactly what was going on and somehow that comforted Maya. "So what is it you're trying to say?" asked Leela.

"The board has decided that future cases where Maya is involved, will not include either you or Dev. Personal relation-ships are to be kept separate from work. Teams will no longer be made up of people related to each other, or in a relationship with each other."

Maya sank into her seat. "Mom and Dad won't be able to work with each other any longer?" She'd noticed Claudia hadn't mentioned Joss's name and Maya wasn't about to bring her attention to her friend.

Claudia shifted her gaze to Maya. "Exactly. In the past, your parents have worked together extremely well. They've been responsible and adhered to the rules of the agency both for their own personal safety and the company as a whole. Now that you are included, some decisions could be made with more consid-eration to you as a daughter than as an agent. We have to consider the emotional impact family relationships will have within each core unit. Emotions can put the entire team in danger. If you had obeyed the rules, worked in harmony with others, this wouldn't have become an issue for consideration. And unfortunately, despite your parent's previous work history, we can't give your parents special dispensation to work together."

Maya got to her feet and began to pace. Then she stopped and turned, staring at Claudia. "How can you do this? You know what you're doing, right? Are you so angry with me that you're happy to take your anger out on my family, on *your* family."

Claudia laughed. "I'm not taking my anger out on my family. I am only doing my job."

Maya snorted. "Keep telling yourself that. You're doing it because you cannot be out in the field with your team. You're so angry about the loss of your ability to walk and everything else that comes with it that you want to take it out on others. Let me tell you something, you can do whatever you like, you can split us up, you can split our family apart. Not gonna make any difference. I'll still do my job to the best of my ability and so will Mom and dad."

Claudia smiled slowly. "That's good to know. I'm sure the board will be happy you're in agreement with their decision."

Dev got to his feet. "Make no mistake. We are not in agreement. And if you think this ends here, you're mistaken."

Claudia rotated the wheelchair with a slight flick of her hands and faced Dev, her neck stiff. "Don't operate under the assumption that you have any kind of power within the organization. Your power died when your daughter began to ride roughshod over our rules."

"So are you going to throw Mother Kali's powers back in her face?"

Claudia shrugged. "Mother Kali gave the power to Maya. What Maya does with it is up to her. And if she does the wrong thing, then I'm not sure who is more to blame, Maya herself, or the goddess who decided to give her that power in the first place."

There was a deep bitterness in her words that made Maya shiver. Claudia was actually angry that the goddess had given Maya power. Instead of her?

No, that couldn't be right.

Kali's powers had been granted to Maya through reincarnation. Perhaps she was just envious of Maya's success rate.

But something else worried Maya. "Is my position within the agency in question?" asked Maya softly.

Claudia was shaking her head now, her expression saying something else entirely. "Of course not. We would never say such a thing. We'd just like to stress that you use your powers more wisely."

Maya was finally beginning to understand what she meant. "No, what you're trying to say is KALIMA wants control over my powers and how I use them."

The smile Maya got from Claudia was enough to confirm her gut had been right. "You don't have to make it sound so bad. We merely want to ensure you don't abuse your powers." Sabala's head shifted beneath Maya's fingers as he got to his feet. Clearly he didn't like what Claude was saying. Maya patted his shoulder and hoped he wouldn't go for Claudia's throat.

"How have I ever abused my powers?"

Claudia shrugged. "We're not saying you have. Yet. Consider it future-proofing."

"That's what I have him here for," said Maya sticking a thumb in Nik's direction. "If KALIMA doesn't want me any longer, who am I to say they're wrong? I still have Nik, and the gods, to support me."

"Look Maya, I'm not saying we want you out. We'd just prefer you don't abuse your position."

Maya shook her head. "I don't think that's what you mean." Maya turned on her heel and headed for the door. She paused and looked over her shoulder at Claudia. "I'm sorry you feel this way. And I'm sorry you had to go to this extent to get back at me. You didn't need to. You could have gone on with your life, with your friends supporting you. Maybe you should rethink what you're doing. We all love you. We still love you. And we know you're hurting. But that doesn't mean you should hurt everyone else around you."

Claudia snorted and straightened, tempering a flicker of fear. The same expression she'd seen on Claudia's face earlier today. What was going on with her? As she stiffened her spine, Maya could see she was stiffening her resolve too.

Had Maya's words weakened Claudia's hold on her hurt and anger? Maya hoped so. Hoped more than anything that her aunt had heard her.

But when Claudia spun the wheelchair around and rolled it toward the door, Maya's heart fell. Claudia paused and the wheelchair came to a stop as she looked at Dev and Leela over her shoulder. They were both still sitting behind the desk looking stunned and hurt.

"The board will be in touch regarding your next cases and how they will be handled. Please don't take any of this personally. It's for everyone's good. Emotional involvement is dangerous. All we're trying to do is to ensure every team works as a cohesive unit."

With that, she turned and rolled toward Maya who stepped aside just in time as Claudia didn't even pause as she rolled through the door.

Claudia looked up at her, giving her a cool smile. "I suggest you take what I've said under advisement. And don't go doing anything rash. Your actions have consequences, even if you don't care about them."

"What consequences?" Maya had to strain to ensure she didn't glance at her parents because she was beginning to suspect what Claudia was implying.

Claudia merely smiled. "Don't jeopardize the positions of your loved ones by doing anything stupid. You're a valuable asset. Remember that."

Then Claudia was rolling down the corridor. But Maya was no longer paying her any attention. She was staring at her parents.

"Tell me you didn't understand that the way I did?" she asked, almost begging.

Dev sat slowly in his chair. "I'm sorry. But I think I understood that exactly as she'd meant it."

Maya returned to her seat, giving Nik a glance to apologize for the family drama. But he didn't seem bothered by it. In fact, he returned to staring at the empty doorway with a strange, almost thoughtful, look on his face.

"Maybe she's only acting on orders?" offered Maya.

Dev shook his head. "I just can't see Edward McCullough doing such a thing to us without consultation, or at least some forewarning."

Maya snorted. "Considering Claudia is family and she managed to spring it on us, I wouldn't have any problem believing McCullough is behind it."

Dev sat back, his eyes dark. "It's all just speculation until we know more."

The silence in the room burgeoned, filled only by the sound of Sabala's soft breathing.

"So what do we do now?" asked Maya.

Leela sighed and rounded the table to sit beside Maya. Maya suspected her mom's legs refused to support her. And she understood how she felt. "I'm so sorry, Mom."

Leela waved her off. "You have nothing to be sorry for,"

"But *I* caused this. If I'd only saved Claudia instead of Stefan, this wouldn't be happening."

"Look Maya, everything we do has consequences."

"And everything we don't do also has consequences," Maya mumbled.

"If this was meant to happen, it would have, no matter what your choice had been."

"You're saying that had I not changed the past and saved Stefan, then this might still be happening, because the board would have seen that as irresponsible too?"

Dev nodded. "Exactly. So, no point in looking back. Or even in questioning Claudia's motives. We need to figure out our next step."

"Which is?"

"You leaving KALIMA."

Sabala huffed and Maya would have shushed him if she wasn't so shocked. "What?" Maya was aghast. "No. I can't do that. Didn't you just hear what Claudia said?"

Leela laughed. "Empty threat, Maya. And even if they throw us out of KALIMA we have enough backers and contacts to keep doing what we're doing without worrying about the board."

"But what about income? You guys can't live on love and air."

Nik shifted. "You don't have to worry about that. You can work on behalf of my father. We have a huge network of people working for us across the globe, and plenty of work to keep you all busy. You can still do Kali's work, but with our support."

"And if KALIMA decides to retaliate when they don't have their asset any longer?"

Nik shrugged. "Guess they'll just have to deal?"

Maya sat back and folded her arms. "This is going to be fun."

CHAPTER 21

MAYA GOT TO her feet, and met her mom's eyes. "Joss?"

"She had some errands to run."

Maya rolled her eyes. "Probably means she had to check on the house for her parents."

Leela shook her head. "They *are* her parents, Maya. There isn't anything we can do about it except take good care of her."

Maya grunted. "It doesn't look like we will be able to take care of her especially considering the danger we're in right now."

Dev smiled, but the expression seemed strained. "Afraid I have to agree with you there. Joss will have to think long and hard before she agrees to continue with us. Of course, she does have a choice."

"What choice?"

"She can choose to remain with KALIMA, or she can come with us."

"And where exactly is 'with us'?" asked Maya wondering what her father had in mind.

"First, I need to download all my data to a safe location. They can't bug the place. The magical wards provide too much interference."

"But they can descend upon the house and confiscate what they deem relevant." Leela's smile was anything but pleasant.

Dev nodded. "They know I'd never abandon my daughter."

"You sure you don't want me to just agree with them and keep working for the agency?" asked Maya. "I still think that's the best idea. At least for now."

Leela shook her head. "It's a matter of principle. And integrity."

Maya snorted. "Principles and integrity can take a flying leap as far as I'm concerned. No offence, Mom. If what I'm doing by leaving KALIMA is going to endanger you guys, then it only makes sense for me to stay."

Dev leaned forward. "Maybe Maya has a point."

Leela glared at him horrified. "Are you insane?"

He smiled, the expression tender and sweet. "No I'm not insane. But I am right. Maybe she should take a case or two, and give us some time to get our things together."

Leela smiled, expression filled with relief as she sank back into the chair. She looked deflated, and Maya knew exactly why. It wasn't unlike what Maya was feeling right now.

The loss of Claudia had gone beyond just a paranoid fear. It was now a permanent thing. Claudia had crossed the line, and she'd been the one to break ties with them. Whatever she'd been up to all these months, she'd done with the single intention of pushing them away.

Maya looked at her dad. "I never understood until now how one small thing could have such big ramifications." He nodded understandingly, his face somber. "One thing that I did would cause such happiness, and at the same time heartbreak. But if I'd done something totally different, that too would have had its consequences. No matter which way we turn all we can do is the best at that point in time. Even hindsight is effed-up."

Maya grinned at her mum apologetically. "Sorry, Mom."

Leela waved her hand. "I completely understand. This whole day has been effed-up," she said with a sigh.

Though surprised, Maya didn't show it. Instead, she got to her feet and glanced up at Nik, wondering if he had anything to contribute. But he had a distant look on his face that told her his mind was elsewhere, deep in thought.

Dev was busy scanning his laptop. He looked up and said, "Maya, if you want to take a case to keep up the pretence, there is one that just came through. It hasn't been picked up yet. Probably because it's applicable to you in particular."

Maya nodded for him to elaborate.

"It's a case down in Mexico. A dancer dead in the small village outside of Nogales. You and Joss would make a legitimate team. And though I may not be able to accompany you on a case, I'm still your Section Chief."

"Okay. I'll take it." She looked up at Nik. "Did you know about this one?"

Nik shook his head. "No. But I'm not surprised. There are a lot of them and some haven't come up on my radar yet. Plus I only just got back to work." He shrugged.

"You want to give me a ride? Or do I have to use public transport for this one?"

Nik smiled. "'Course I'll give you a ride. Come, we'd better go. You just never know when I'm going to get called back."

Maya was walking out the door when her Dad called her name. She looked back at him. "We'll start looking at possible places to go to. We definitely have to leave this house. We might have to take Nik up on his offer at some stage. But for now, everything will continue as it is. You just take care of the case and take care of yourself."

"Don't do anything stupid." Her mom had to add that in, but Maya understood why she was reiterating Claudia's words. This is what had got them in the situation in the first place. Claudia was right. It was all Maya's fault.

Maya's fault for wanting to do things her way. Maya's fault for being rebellious.

Maya's fault for wanting to be the hero.

She'd gotten way ahead of herself, perhaps too fond of the idea of saving the day, more than being part of a successful team. Something twisted in her gut as she began to wonder if Claudia had a point.

But she wasn't ready to say it yet. And to be honest she wasn't sure she'd ever be ready.

But the look on Claudia's face stuck in Maya's memory. Fear. What would she be afraid of? Maybe she knew her actions would drive her family away from her. That was probably it. Maya didn't have a choice in the matter.

As she turned to leave, she stopped again and glanced at her father. "Considering where we're at with KALIMA, can you maybe find out where Ria is right now? What if we leave and then lose touch with her. And what if she wants to be with us instead?"

Dev nodded. "I know exactly where she is. I'll get in touch. She's unlikely to know what's going on. Of course, she will also have the right to make the decision that's best for her. Don't go expecting her to choose you over the agency, okay? Remember that they gave her a place to hide, a new face and a new life."

Maya nodded. She was well aware of where they stood, well aware Ria may not side with them. She gave a sad sigh. "I know, and I don't expect her to agree with us. I just thought she had a right to know, and a right to make the decision herself. We still haven't seen her yet, so we have no idea what she's thinking."

Dev nodded. "Don't worry about it. I'll get that all sorted while you attend to this case."

He rummaged inside one of his drawers and withdrew a plastic bag.

Reaching out to Maya he said, "Pesos. You may need it. It's not much, but it's just in case." He paused as Maya took the bag, weighing the nomination of notes and coins in her palm. "Make sure you take Sabala with you. And be careful, okay?"

Maya nodded solemnly, not in the mood for any smart remarks. "About Joss. Technically she is family."

Her mom laughed. "Good point. But since Claudia only mentioned personal family, and she didn't say friends, I think you're good. If they ask any questions, you can just pretend ignorance. "

Maya shook her head. "If I didn't know any better, Mom, I'd say you were enjoying all the subterfuge. Pulling the wool over KALIMA's eyes suddenly looking like a lot of fun?"

Her dad huffed. "As much as it may feel like fun, don't forget they can be dangerous if they want to. They have agents out there who have no qualms about being merciless."

Maya frowned. "KALIMA has mercenary agents?"

He nodded. "I've never agreed with this part of the business. But the rest of the board always thought it necessary. Especially when the need arose to take out a demon long distance. We have a group of mercenaries consisting mostly of snipers and bombers. The problem with them is they've grown to see little difference between humans and demons, mostly because the demon targets bear human guises."

Leela got to her feet. "I think you've forgotten the part where the board decided to hire mercenaries who are able to kill demons with human faces because they're more bloodthirsty than your average assassin. They needed harder men. Then, we understood the reasoning behind it, but as time went on the mercenaries they hired were more dangerous, and less controllable."

Maya shook her head. "Can this get any worse?"

～

MAYA AND NIK ran into Joss in the hallway. Sabala was right at Maya's side, where' he'd been all through the last horrible hour.

Joss had a rucksack pulled over her shoulder and it seemed to be weighing her down. Nik reached for it and she gave him a grateful smile. "Thanks. That damned bag was heavier than I expected. Should have known better than to throw all those clothes into one bag." She rolled her shoulders and then looked from Maya to Nik, and then back again. "What's going on?" she asked, a suspicious look on her face.

Maya sighed and went to her friend, curling her arm around her shoulders. "So, we had this visit from a certain ex-friend, who basically told us we are all about to be ex-agents."

Joss's mouth dropped open and she stopped to stare at Maya.

"Shut the front door." She paused. Narrowing her eyes, she said, "Don't tell me. Claudia."

Maya laughed. "Good guess."

But Joss was shaking her head. "Nope. I could see that happening a mile away."

The hellhound expelled a burst of air through his nose, clearly agreeing with Joss. Maya ignored him, asking Joss, "You could?" as they began to walk up the stairs. "How come you never mentioned anything to me?"

She shrugged. "Not exactly the type of thing one would mention to a friend who is hurting. I know what you guys went through. And I know how guilty you felt after Claudia was injured. Sometimes, no matter how much you tell someone something they don't listen to you because it's their own pain that's blocking them."

Maya grinned. "You sure you're not a reincarnated priestess of Wisdom?"

Joss snorted. "No I'm not. But I certainly could give one a run for her money."

She looked over her shoulder, and they noticed Nik was still standing at the bottom of the stairs staring at his cellphone.

"So he's back to staring at that thing twenty-four-seven?"

Maya had gotten used to it. And said as much.

But her friend shook her head. "I'm sure it must be enjoyable dating a guy who is permanently on his cell phone." At Maya's glare Joss rolled her eyes. "Okay fine, I know you guys have a special sort of relationship that precludes jealousy and possessiveness. I'm just not sure if I could be like you.

Maya punched her lightly on her shoulder. "That's the last thing we need to be thinking about right now. Get ready. We're going to Mexico."

CHAPTER 22

*J*OSS RAISED an eyebrow. "That's a first. Usually you don't want me to come with you."

Maya huffed as she tugged the doors of her closet open and began to change. The bottom of her boots were still stained red with blood from the scene in the theatre. She sank to the floor and untied the laces, chucking the boots into a corner before Joss could see their condition.

Maya really wasn't in the mood to have Joss interrogating her about the dead girl. But as she rummaged through her clothes in the closet. The sight of the blood caking her fingernails made her spin on her heel and head straight into the bathroom.

She turned on the faucet and began to soap her hands.

Ever since she'd had the dream she'd felt off balance, as if a strange energy tugged at her from deep within. But she'd kept it to herself, afraid it would only make them worry.

Not so long ago on that stage in London, Maya had felt the pull of that energy again.

Her stomach twinged just the tiniest bit. It must mean something, but she didn't want to borrow trouble. Surely the effect would fade.

No doubt the dream would continue to affect her more so because she'd seen death first hand, experienced it as if it had been her own.

She'd tried not to think about what those girls had been through, how they'd died, how they'd suffered before they had died. She had to deal with the pain of it herself. Just until she managed to figure it out.

She shouldn't be feeling guilt. She knew that.

She'd done nothing to contribute to the girl's pain. And yet she still felt responsible.

As if being privy to their agony had made their pain a part of her.

She scrubbed her nails until her fingers turned red, until every last fleck of blood had been removed, then dried off and headed back into her room to throw on jeans and a comfortable shirt. Joss was sitting on Maya's bed, tapping away at her laptop. Not the one she used to do her home-school work.

Her agency laptop.

Maya stared at her, at the packed bag sitting at the foot of her bed, at Maya's wallet and cellphone that sat beside each other so she wouldn't forget on the way out. Maya stood where she was, pulling her jacket on and said, "Joss, there's something you should know."

Joss glanced up, a little distracted as she tried to read the screen and pay attention to Maya at same time. Maya waited until she focused solely on her.

"Claudia didn't get just my parents in trouble. *You* are included too. The new rule is no team shall comprise of people who are in a personal relationship." Joss's eyes widened. "Claudia mentioned family, and she only mentioned personal relationships in passing. So I suspect I can get away with pleading ignorance if we get into trouble. But I thought it was only fair you know about this before we leave. And then you make your own decision."

"And what decision is that?" asked Joss, a strange edge to her voice.

"As to whether you want to defy the orders of the agency and come with me. I think there will come a point where you'll have to make a decision about where your support lies. They may ask you to choose."

"Why would they?" Joss's cheeks were pink, and going another shade darker.

"In case we decide to do something that's against the rules," Maya said as a ripple of fear ran through her.

What if Joss just turned around and went straight to Claudia? Maya shook her head. She couldn't let herself believe Joss was capable of such betrayal.

Joss rolled her eyes. "It doesn't matter what you do. Even if you break the rules, you know I'll support you and your family no matter what." Joss stopped and stared at Maya with narrowed eyes. "Did you think I wouldn't?"

"Of course not. But I didn't want to expect you to do something wrong just for us."

Joss snorted and got to her feet, dropping the laptop on her bed. "If it came down to it, a choice between KALIMA and you, I'd choose you any day. As far as I'm concerned you are family. Short of being a serial killer, and even then I would probably help you hide from the authorities, there isn't very much reason anyone can give me."

Maya blinked away tears, and smiled as they walked to the door. She glanced over her shoulder at the laptop. "Aren't you taking that?"

Joss shook her head. "Absolutely not. For all I know, there's a tracking device on it. I'd rather leave it here."

Maya laughed. "Joss, we are taking a KALIMA case. We're not making a run for it."

With a nod Joss said, "It doesn't make a difference. Now that I know what they're capable of, I don't feel very comfortable with them knowing exactly where I am and what I'm doing."

Heading out the door, Maya had to laugh softly. She should have expected Joss's reaction.

The sharp clacking on the wood floor told Maya that Sabala followed close behind them.

Joss turned and looked at the hellhound. "Are you coming with?"

"Of course, he is. He's likely going to be our only protection. I have a feeling Nik won't have time to hang around. He's going to just give us a ride. The border of Mexico is hardly the place to be without protection."

Joss's eyebrows reached for her hairline. "Maya, I like to live dangerously, but what the hell are you thinking?"

"Don't worry. We have a contact across the border who will take us to the location. There's another dead dancer and we want to make sure this is one of ours first before we make any assumptions about how widespread the deaths are."

"Oh for the love of Mother Kali."

Maya couldn't help the laughter erupting from her lips. She managed to suppress it enough to turn it into a hacking cough but Joss glared at her.

"What?"

Maya cleared her throat as she saw Nik tucking the tablet into a small messenger bag which he slung over his shoulder. "I don't think Kali would appreciate such profanity."

"Profanity?" Joss scoffed. "That wasn't profanity."

"Well it was disrespectful."

Joss snorted. "Let Kali be the judge of that."

"Joss," admonished Maya.

Maya didn't have the chance to respond as Nik arrived beside them and gave them an expectant glance. "You ladies ready?"

Maya nodded. "Only thing I'm worried about is our Madus and knives aren't going to fend off a hail of bullets."

Nik looked amused. "Give me a moment. I'll be back with guns and ammo." Then he was gone and Maya and Joss exchanged a curious glance as they waited.

He returned within seconds bearing a small metal box, which he lay on the floor. He flipped the lid and the girls peered inside.

Joss snorted. "Awesome. We have fire. We have guns. What more could a girl ask for."

CHAPTER 23

NIK HELD OUT his hands, and Joss and Maya took one each and held on tight. The first thing Maya noticed was that Sabala, who had travelled on his own, hadn't appeared beside Nik and the two girls when they materialized.

"Where's the pooch?" she whispered to Nik.

Nik's startled expression sent a quiver of fear through Maya. "Let me check." Nik shuttered his eyes and concentrated, using his demigod powers to find out what was keeping Sabala. When Nik exhaled, Maya's stomach tightened.

Something was wrong.

"He can't travel here. Something is keeping him away."

"Like what?" hissed Maya, annoyed. They'd arrived near the back wall of an old hut that looked about ready to fall down around their ears.

Nik shook his head. "I won't know until I go back and speak to him. It could be any number of things including a magical ward."

Joss's eyes widened. "Here? In Mexico?"

He nodded. "Every culture has spells and rituals that allow them to keep demons out of specific areas."

"So something is going on here that people don't want demons or people with magic, to see."

"Exactly." Nik's worried tone put Maya on edge. Could this get any worse?

She scanned the hut. The place was made with mud and straw, with a roof that seemed to have been thrown together from random pieces of metal. Maya squinted and could have sworn the ceiling materials were flattened gasoline cans.

She sank to the ground beside Nik and Joss. The little abandoned village was situated a few miles outside of Nogales, near the tourist hotspot of Merida. It sat on the outskirts of Mexico, on a long stretch of land that led to the US border. Because of its location, it had long been controlled by drug and gun runners. Likely also by slave runners too.

Maya wondered what danger lay outside, and hoped that Nik wouldn't leave them alone too long.

Nik held his phone between the three of them and Maya studied the screen which held a small map of the town.

He stabbed the screen, aiming at a hut on the outer edge of the town. "This is where we are now. And this," he pointed further south, "is the discovery site."

Both girls nodded, and Maya wondered whether her friend's heart was beating as hard as hers. She was about to encounter another dead girl and there wasn't a single cell in her body that welcomed the thought.

Maya automatically looked for a pair of glassy obsidian eyes, which would appear seemingly unimpressed with the drama of the day. But Sabala wasn't there and she felt her stomach twist with disappointment. She'd gotten way too used to having the hellhound around.

He seemed to know everything, seemed to understand her emotions too. She'd grown so close to him, that now, just the thought of losing him made her heart hurt.

"We'll find the girl and see what else our contact can tell us. Let's hope this isn't connected."

Nik nodded. "Just be careful. I have to go. Wait here for fifteen minutes, and a man will come to find you. His name is Pedro Alvarez, and he's a village elder. He'll translate if you find the girl's family."

Maya nodded and hugged Nik, holding him tightly for a few short moments.

Then Nik straightened and said, "I'll be back as soon as possible. You don't have to worry. If you need me, just text me."

Maya nodded.

She had to now get used to seeing less of Nik, and as much as she'd been so calm about it with Joss, she knew it would be hard. But she was strong enough. If she wanted to be with him she'd have to be strong enough.

Nik disappeared into nothing. As soon as he left, Maya turned to Joss. They both sank into a crouch, huddling together in the darkness as they waited. Half a dozen windows cut into the adobe walls, covered by scraps of fabric that did a terrible job of hiding the night sky.

Somewhere in the distance a coyote cried, the call sending a ripple of unease down Maya's spine.

Thankfully, before Maya got any more anxious, they heard the shuffle-scrape of shoes outside the door. It was a poor excuse for protection. A few pieces of wood nailed to a few pieces of metal, providing a very fragile seal to the hut.

Maya had to wonder who lived here, how anyone could live in an almost-bare space? A low cot covered in filthy blankets, a gas heater and a small gas stove occupied a rickety table. A battered metal pot and small stack of plastic plates, cups and utensils sat beside the stove.

Maya understood what poverty might feel like. She also understood that the life that she lived was one of indescribable privilege compared to this.

She blinked as the metal of the door groaned and squeaked. The girls hurried across the small hut and backed up against the wall behind the door, both wary just in case their visitor was a danger to them. Maya's hands were at the ready, the fire pulsing beneath her palm.

The door swung open slowly, the moonlight casting a long shadow of the man into the room. Maya couldn't make much out of him, or his distorted shadow.

He hunched over and peered inside the dark interior. "Are you here?" His voice was scratchy and hoarse.

He took another step inside, and as soon as he was out of reach of the door, Maya pushed it shut. The man whirled, his shocked - and slightly disappointed - expression stark against his gaunt features as he stared at the two girls.

With a hand over his heart, he took a few sharp breaths. Maya felt extremely guilty for giving him such a fright.

"Who are you?" she asked, deciding to be safe instead of sorry.

The man squinted, studying her from head to toe. "They send *you*?"

He was not impressed.

Maya frowned. "Who are you?" she asked again, wondering whether he understood English.

"Pedro Alvarez. My contact . . . he was sending someone to help us with our . . . problem."

"Who is your contact?" Maya asked, just being careful in case this was a trap.

"Dev Rao."

Maya sighed, and released a breath. She gave the old man a smile. "I'm Maya. I'm Dev's daughter."

The old man reached out to shake her hand. His skin was papery, his hands fleshless and thin.

Maya was acutely aware that Pedro came from this land filled with poverty.

He took a step back and studied the two girls. "He send me his daughter?" the old man said narrowing his eyes. "And who are you?" he asked Joss.

Joss smiled. "I think you could say I'm his adopted daughter."

The man looked at Maya and she agreed with a vigorous nod. At this moment, all Maya wanted was to get the job done and head back home.

"Señor, can you show us what you need help with?"

Pedro gave a short nod, as if he understood now that they were down to business. "Come with me."

Joss and Maya exchanged glances, they really didn't have much of a choice. This man had been vetted by her father, surely she could trust him. He led them out the hut keeping low, remaining in the shadows. They carried along the wall for half a dozen huts, and Maya worried the bright light of the moon would bring their movements to attention if anyone was watching from the hillside.

But the old man didn't seem bothered by this. At last his progress slowed and he pushed aside a ragged curtain shielding the doorway of a large hut. He slipped inside and Maya and Joss followed, their eyes adjusting to the darkness within. Near the left wall lay the body of a young girl. A small kerosene lamp burned in the far corner, providing a soft glow that made the corpses skin strangely animated. It also illuminated the floor of the hut, bringing the streaks of blood patterning the hard packed floor into start contrast.

The girl's black, low-heeled shoes glistened with blood and Maya wondered what kind of damage she'd see if she removed them. The injuries were bad enough with bare feet. Was it any better in closed shoes?

Maya moved forward but the old man hissed, snapping a hand out to block her from getting closer.

She took his hand in hers and patted the back of his wrist. "Don't worry. I'll be fine."

The man looked over at Joss, as if needing reassurance. He must have received it because he let go and took a step back.

Maya sank to her knees beside the girl trying not to look at her ruined feet. Her heart was thundering in her chest and she had to take a moment to calm herself down. After a few seconds, she pulled the energy from her fire and reached out with her mind for a heartbeat.

She didn't find one.

Again she tried to locate some form of corresponding energy within the body. This time she did feel a hint of pulsing. A residual pulse of life. Maya had learned a while ago that touching a body gave her a sense of the life within. And that the soul did remain within the body for a short time. Could Maya access the girl's memories?

But gradually, the pulsing drew Maya's attention away from her thoughts, calling her like a siren.

The beat of drums. The haunting call of a violin. The chink of cymbals.

CHAPTER 24

aya took a deep breath and focused, pulling her mind from the entrancing music.

Maya glanced again at Pedro. "Do you know who this girl is?"

Maya got to her feet and walked to the old man. She took his hand in hers and said softly, "I understand how you feel. This place is dangerous. I don't want to put you in any trouble. We just want to know what happened to her."

The old man paled, despite the brown of his weathered leathery skin. "But you come to find the killer?"

"My first job is to find out how this poor girl died." Maya could tell he was relieved when she didn't stress a desire to find out who killed the girl.

Maya glanced over her shoulder at the body. She looked young, possibly in her mid-teens. Her red ruffled dress and black square heeled shoes confirmed she was a flamenco dancer which seemed unusual in such a desolate town. But one never knew where the desire to dance will spark. Poverty didn't preclude talent.

"Somewhere in this village is a mother who is looking for her daughter. Or siblings who are looking for their sister. How can we not let them know what happened to her?"

Pedro took a small, hesitant step towards the body. "You will not look for killer? You promise?"

Maya blinked. "If that is what her family wants then we won't tell the authorities. I promise."

Maya glanced up at Joss and recognised the conflicting emotions in her friend's eyes. They reflected her own.

"Yes," said Joss moving to sit beside the man. "She's telling you the truth. She won't call the police. You all will be safe."

Maya glanced at Joss gratefully. She'd been uncertain, worried Joss may not support her. "Do you recognize her?"

The old man nodded at last, although he still looked terrified.

Maya moved to stand beside him. "Could you find her family for us?"

"Si. But they may not come. They are scared."

Nodding, Maya said, "I understand. But please let them know we promised to keep them safe. All we want to know is what happened and the information will not go to the police."

Pedro nodded, satisfied. "*Si*. I go."

Maya's heart beat faster. She prayed the old man would return soon with the girl's family.

CHAPTER 25

A SMALL COMMOTION at the door announced the arrival of the girl's family. The pure grief on the woman's face broke Maya's heart.

Maya moved towards the girl's head, making space for the mother and a younger girl to sit beside her. The woman didn't look much older than Maya's mother, and yet her skin was weathered and brown, her body emaciated.

The girl standing next to her was around ten years old, just as thin as her mother.

Neither paid Maya or Joss any attention. They had eyes only for the dead girl.

And Maya understood completely.

She and Joss weren't here for gratitude. They'd come to do the right thing for the girl.

The mother spoke softly to her daughter, and though Maya didn't understand her words, she still felt her eyes burn with tears.

Maya glanced up at Pedro and gave a slight shake of her head. With relief she saw him whisper to the old woman and child. Whatever he said made the mother cry harder, but he patted her back softly, spoke again in her ear. Then she nodded, holding a hand to her eyes as she cried for her daughter.

She got to her feet slowly, dragging the girl with her to stand near the open doorway.

Maya looked over at Pedro. "Can you ask the mother what the girl's name is?"

He nodded and spoke to the woman in Spanish.

"*¿Cuál es su nombre?*"

The woman answered, her words halting and filled with grief. "Rosario Chavez."

Pedro didn't need to translate that. Maya asked, "What was she doing here?"

The old man spoke.

"*¿Qué estaba haciendo aquí?*"

And the woman responded. "*Ella estaba practicando para el proceso del día de los metros en Mérida.*"

"She was practicing for the Dia de los Metros process in Merida." Pedro spoke wiht sad old eyes.

Maya nodded. "That's the nearest town." Pedro nodded. "Could you ask her if she knows anyone who would hurt her daughter . . . Rosario?"

Pedro shifted his old eyes to the mother.

"*¿Sabe de alguien que quiera lastimar a su hija?*"

The woman responded in a rush of tearful words, and Pedro shifted his gaze to Maya. "She says no. Rosa . . . she was hard-working. A good girl. All she wanted was to dance."

The woman began to cry and Maya nodded at Pedro to let them go. As they left, she turned her attention back to Rosario. Since the family couldn't answer Maya's questions maybe the girl still could. Maya had felt the pulse of life within her. It meant Maya could attempt to access the girl's memories if not her actual past.

Although Maya had performed time jumps like this before, she'd never done it on the recently departed.

She motioned to Joss to come closer. "I'm going to try a time jump," Maya whispered. "If anything goes wrong, text Nik to come help."

"Do you think that's wise?"

"It's our only hope of knowing what happened to her. I only have a small window of opportunity because the longer she is dead the less likely it will be for me to access her memories."

Maya's tone caused Joss to clamp her jaw shut, and she knew her friend wasn't happy. But Joss also understood what they needed. And Maya was grateful she didn't protest.

Closing her eyes, she concentrated on Rosario. Maya relaxed and focused her thoughts on the girl the same way she'd done with Kas when she'd accessed his memories in order to save Lord Yama and Nik.

This time though, the person whose thoughts she accessed was dead and she had so little time left. As she breathed she concentrated on Rosa, slowly able to sense the energy she gave off. Maya followed the energy, timing her heart beat with the pulsing emanating from the girl.

Riding the energy Maya focused on Rosa's face and followed it into the girl's mind. Almost immediately Maya saw the hut again, but this time from a different perspective. She, Rosa, was moving and the room spun around her. Maya could feel the movement she made, twirling, stamping her feet, sweeping her skirt this way and that.

But the movements were frenzied, not passionate. Rosa's emotions were tumultuous, not serene. Fear filled her veins and made her want to stop but she had no control.

Images filled her mind. Faces of people surrounding the girl, some joyful, some hard and angry. People from her life maybe. Maya was concentrating hard on recognizing faces she almost didn't see the one face that made her heart go cold.

Claudia.

Maya shook the thought from her head. No. Of course, the

woman wasn't Claudia. Maya had just thought it was her. Maybe her residual anger at her aunt had summoned an image of her.

Maya let out a pained gasp. It was the dream all over again, only a different girl and a different dance form.

When Maya opened her eyes Joss and Pedro were both staring at her, Joss curious, the old man confused.

"What is it?" asked Joss.

"It's just like London."

Joss's face said she'd suspected as much. Maya reached out to close the girl's cloudy eyes. Pain lanced through her fingers and energy bit at her.

"Get away," hissed Maya as her fire surged out of her in response. "Somethings wrong."

Joss stared at Maya's hand, at the flame spurting from her fingertips. Then, as if taken possession by her own inner demon, she pushed to her feet and stumbled around the body, grabbing hold of Pedro and pulling him away. The old man protested, and Maya wondered what he was saying.

"There's no time for water, Señor," Joss said as she bustled him out of the room.

Joss would stand guard at the door and refuse to let anyone inside. That left Maya to concentrate on the job at hand. The fire thrust against her, driving deeper into her flesh. Maya was at a loss as to what to do. What the hell was going on here and what was this strange power that existed within Rosa's body?

For a moment, fear surged through her.

Maya blinked.

Swallowing hard, she gritted her teeth and pushed the pain deeper within herself.

She brought the fire up through her muscles to the surface of her skin, and soon she was ablaze. Red hot heat floated from her body, and a distant part of her mind registered that she'd just burnt off all her clothes.

But she didn't have time to pay any attention to her nudity.

Rosa's energy no longer held Maya captive. She had to put all her concentration into her fire, and burn the body to cinders.

She bit down on her teeth, pulling more fire to the surface. Any onlooker would see a human on fire. Something maybe scarier than even a demon would be.

Thankfully, in this part of the world, the chance of a fire engine coming their way was pretty low.

The body of Rosa Chavez was on fire, the flames burning brighter and hotter than most crematoriums.

And Maya was burning too.

She wasn't afraid. In fact, she welcomed the heat and the flame.

She waited, sending more fire deep within Rosa's body, afraid for the people in the village who may be hurt by whatever energy possessed the corpse.

Outside, she could hear the low rumble of a crowd, concerned cries of the people from the village now gathering outside. She could even hear Joss's voice warning people to stay away.

With one last sigh, Maya took a step back from the burning body. She moved away one step at a time as the fire began to die down.

The spirit of the girl was gone, passed over to Patala or wherever her heart and faith led her. At least she was now in peace. Maya hoped.

As she neared the doorway, she heard Joss's voice through the confusion in her mind.

"Stay where you are." Joss's tone was strange as she stood in the open doorway.

"Why?" All Maya wanted was to get out of the hut and away from the remains.

But Joss just shook her head.

"Because you're buck-naked, that's why."

CHAPTER 26

DESPITE THE HEAT within the hut, Maya felt a shiver run down her spine. The first time she'd burst into flame, she'd been mortally embarrassed. Nik had pushed her far during that session of training, and she'd exploded into a ball of fire incinerating all her clothing.

It wasn't exactly the way a girl wanted to get naked with her guy.

Nik had been the perfect gentleman, handing her his jacket and turning away until she was clothed.

Right now, she concentrated on grabbing the rucksack Joss threw at her. She sank to a crouch and rummaged inside pulling out a change of clothes. Of course, she'd come prepared.

A girl never knew when she'd burn her clothing off with a sudden burst of spontaneous combustion.

Good thing not too many people had to live with her problem.

She was shrugging on her jacket when Joss hissed, "Hurry up and get some clothes on. We have incoming."

Maya zipped her coat up. Hurrying to the door she hitched

the rucksack high on her shoulder. As she thrust aside the fabric curtain Maya's heart jumped into her throat.

She was staring down the barrel of a very menacing looking gun.

She let out a shocked gasp, and the weapon drew closer, stopping an inch from her nose. The gunman studied her from over-the-top of the barrel. The expression in his eyes made her stomach go cold.

This was no village elder. There was a hard coldness in the man's expression. She and Joss were in deep trouble.

And it was too late to call Nik to their aid.

Damn it all to Patala and back.

Beside her, she felt Joss shift closer, curling her fingers through her elbow. Maya could feel the blood rushing through her friend's veins as her heart sped up, just as fast as Maya's.

The man spoke, his voice guttural and threatening as he stared at Maya and Joss. *"¿Quién eres tú? ¿Cuál es tu negocio aquí?"*

But Maya didn't understand a word. And Joss, it appeared, choose to feign ignorance too. Instead she huddled close to translate in Maya's ear.

Pedro called out from across a clearing, where a dozen armed men kept the villagers at bay.

"The thug's name is Luis."

Pedro glared at Luis. *"¿Qué es lo que quieres con esas chicas?"*

"Pedro is asking him what he wants with us."

Luis turned on Pedro, his expression now suspicious. Maya wished the old man had not intervened.

Luis waved his weapon and one of his thugs stepped toward Pedro. The man was swarthy, with dark oily air and beady black eyes. He wore a sleeveless tank that revealed arms covered in tattoos that were hard to see from a distance.

The thug reached for the old man. *"Cállate, viejo sucio,"* he growled, ramming the barrel of his gun into the back of his head.

Although Pedro crumpled to the ground, Maya was relieved. She'd rather him unconscious than dead.

Now she had the sole attention of Luis, she didn't have much choice. If he threatened her, she'd have to kill him, human or not. The fact that he was waving a gun in her face, who for all he knew was just an innocent girl, told her he wouldn't hesitate to pull the trigger.

Maya cleared her throat. "Please . . . what do you want?"

Luis's face was hidden, the moonlight shining from behind him outlining his bare skull.

He took a step closer to Maya, and she made out the craggy lines of his face, the perfect white teeth, and the prettiest cornflower-blue eyes Maya had ever seen.

Talk about life not being fair.

"I think the correct question is 'what do you want' little girl?" he responded in perfect English.

Maya shook her head.

"We were just travelling through. Came to help with the fire," said Joss.

Maya's stomach tightened, wishing Joss hadn't brought attention to herself. With Maya's dark coloring she could possibly pass as Latina, but with Joss's pale blonde hair and equally pale skin, she stood out in this crowd.

And from Luis's expression as he sneered at Maya, they were in deeper trouble. He studied Joss from head to toe, spending considerable time at bust and crotch. The guy was an absolute creep, and Maya wanted to punch him in the face.

"I know something else you might want to help us with," he said, his eyes dark and malevolent.

Maya shook her head. "Our family will be looking. We'd better be going. If we don't get back soon they'll call the police."

A few of the men began to laugh, the sound resonating amongst the crowd.

She was about to speak when Luis pointed the gun at her face again, and played with the trigger. He held it in a nonchalant way, horizontal gangster style, which made Maya feel more threatened.

In a flash, Luis reached out and grabbed hold of Joss's throat, pressing a thumb against the front of her neck. Joss choked and sputtered, and grabbed his hand, trying to pull his fingers away from her neck.

Nothing worked, and Maya felt impotent.

She wasn't sure what to do. She had to entice Luis into the hut with her. That was the only way they'd be able to get away with a small chance of survival.

Maya laughed, trying to sound extremely bitchy. "Trust me, you don't want her." She injected enough derision into the word.

Joss glared at her, already onto what Maya was attempting.

Luis shifted his predatory gaze towards Maya. "What do you mean?"

"All I mean is, she's probably slept with every guy in the school. I know for a fact that she is HIV positive. You definitely don't want to risk sleeping with her." Maya swallowed the bile rising in her throat, accompanying words she'd never say about her friend.

She reminded herself this was an act. She was playing a part.

Luis looked at her. "What you trying to say? You just spoiling my fun with this one, so what do I get in place of her?"

Maya lifted her chin, staring at him. "How about me?"

Luis raised an eyebrow. "What's so special about you?" He stared suspiciously, his gaze raking her head to toe, in much the same way as h'd scanned Joss only moments ago.

"I haven't been with anybody. Ever."

The grin spreading across his face made Maya want to shiver. She'd hit the jackpot in terms of offers. He let go of Joss, and Maya squeezed her friend's hand, pulling her close.

"Maya what the hell are you doing?" Joss hissed. Maya just waved her into silence.

"I very much like that offer, little girl," said Luis as he stepped closer to Maya. She took three steps back, further into the hut, which made the thug grin wider. He assumed *he* was the one pushing her into the room so he could have his fun.

He was wrong.

When the doorway filled with curious faces, Maya turned her attention back to him. "Do you mind if we don't have an audience?" she asked softly, giving the door a glance.

Luis sneered, and appeared to be considering her request. He glanced at the door and the lascivious expressions of his men. Then he swore at them and waved them away. When they didn't move he took two threatening steps towards them and yelled louder. He achieved more success with threatened violence than the simple request.

The men faded into the darkness outside.

Luis turned his full attention on Maya, completely ignoring that she'd taken a few more steps back. She now had the smoldering corpse of the poor dancer in her sight, the smell enough to make anyone want to throw up.

But, given the situation she was in right now, any girl would want to vomit. Despite her show of courage to Joss, Maya was terrified.

She'd done this once before. Which was probably why Joss had given her such a horrified look. The last time she was also alone with a guy. The only difference was then she'd accidentally burned him to smithereens and he turned out to be a demon. Now, she faced a man, a flesh-and-blood human, who had the very same intention.

And Maya was going to have to take drastic measures to save herself and her friend.

Luis took one step towards her, and sniffed. His attention was drawn away by the heated embers at the middle of the hut.

"Did you put out the fire?" he asked, curious as his gaze returned to Maya's face. It didn't stay there long, drifting lower immediately to scan her body. She could almost hear the thoughts in his head.

He seemed so comfortable with attacking young girls. He must do this often. And had little opposition too.

Just that knowledge made Maya want to dig his eyes out. Only God knew how many women he'd attacked in his lifetime. How many women had suffered at his hands.

Maya nodded, even though he wasn't looking at her. "Yes."

He looked at her suspicious now. "How did you put it out?"

Maya shrugged. "Water," she said. "How else?"

He took a step towards her. "I don't see any water bottles. Where did you get the water from? Not from this village. Because we, *I*, control the water here."

He poked a slender finger at his chest, harder than was necessary. Maya supposed the force with which he stabbed himself was meant to convince her of his power.

It did convince her. And it certainly didn't impress her.

Maya's back was almost to the wall when he took another step. She had nowhere to go now. He reached out and placed a hand around her neck. "Something tells me you are lying."

Maya shook her head, although the movement was difficult, what with his fingers wrapped around her neck.

"I'm not lying. The truth. We had water bottles in our pack."

"Then where are they now," he asked, pushing his face close to hers, his breath wafting over her face.

Maya hesitated then looked back at the smoldering pallet. "I think we threw the bottles into the fire." It was the first thing that came to mind. Although it made absolutely no sense. "I wasn't thinking."

She injected fear into her voice, and began to shiver, hoping to convince him she was merely a weak female.

Maya was ready.

More than ready.

His hand drifted down to her chest, grabbed her breast and

squeezed hard. Her anger was so volatile it took little effort for Maya to grab hold of her fire from and bring it to the surface.

Heat simmered in her body, and she smelled burning flesh. Luis hissed and grabbed his hand back, blowing hard on his burned palm.

"What the-"

He stared at his hand and then looked back up at Maya.

"What the hell was that?" Luis asked.

CHAPTER 27

*L*UIS SWORE, spit flying from his mouth.

Now his shock had worn off, the nerves would be screaming out in pain. It would get worse as the pain of the burn took hold.

He didn't turn and run as Maya had hoped. Instead, his anger spurred him towards her and he reached for her throat again. Despite the heat she was generating he still squeezed hard enough for Maya to fear passing out.

She lifted her knee, slamming it hard between his legs but he merely grunted and squeezed harder. A fist to his midsection did nothing either. What type of man was this? She couldn't fight him off with only her hands and legs.

She had no choice now but to use her fire, though she still hesitated.

He would kill Maya if she didn't do anything.

With a surge of energy, Maya pushed a fresh burst of fire to the palms of her hands. She shoved Luis hard against his chest, her fear and frustration giving the push a burst of power she hadn't intended. She didn't have time to appreciate it though, as she felt the skin at her neck break as his nails gouged into her throat.

But she didn't care about pain.

Luis groaned and fell to the ground, the ball of fire flying past him. He rolled over and sprang back up to his feet. A lithe, smooth move.

Was Luis more than human?

No. That wasn't possible. Her senses hadn't pegged him as anything more. He was just one hardened mother.

Maya wanted to laugh.

Joss would be proud of her thoughts.

He got to his feet, screaming with pain. Maya glanced at the door, terrified his men would come running in to check on him. When nothing happened, her fear ratcheted up another notch. If his men hadn't come running on hearing Luis's screams, they must know he was capable of extraordinary violence.

Maya put all her power behind the next surge of fire that flew from the tips of her fingers. She flinched as her fire hit him straight in the face. For the first time in all the months of fighting, of using her fire in battles just like this, Maya was unable to watch as the man was engulfed by the flames.

He screamed louder, frantically hitting the flames that burned along his chest and neck. His bloodcurdling screams brought the sound of running feet.

Guess his men knew the nuances of his screams to know Luis was not simply enjoying himself now.

Maya looked at Joss, giving her a short nod.

"Nik."

Joss scrambled for her phone sending the text at high speed but seconds went by and Nik hadn't arrived.

They watched as Luis burned, as his men crashed into the room and stared in horror as their boss went up in flames. There was nothing in the room, no blankets, no water to help them put the fire out. A few fled, probably in search of some, while a handful remained, as if keeping watch.

From some of their expressions, the death of their boss didn't seem to be too upsetting. In fact, two of the thugs were smiling, their expressions assessing and opportunistic.

Where one head dies, two more will grow.

Maya had never understood the full meaning of that phrase until today.

People sucked.

It was too late for Luis.

The fire raged, eating at his body, melting all the flesh from his bones. And by the time his men returned with blankets and water, all that remained was a husk of blackened skin.

As the fire sputtered out, the men looked around the hut, curious. They'd seen Luis enter with two girls. And now, he was burnt to a crisp.

For Maya and Joss, the trouble had only just begun.

The men spotted the girls huddled in the corner and ran for them. Maya threw fireballs at them and while they shouted and dusted flames off their clothes she spun around and aimed her fire at the back wall.

Maya had no idea how heat reacted with mud but she sure as hell hoped it meant they'd be able to kick it down and escape.

"Maya!" Joss's urgent yell sent Maya running instinctively at the wall, pulling Joss with her. They slammed hard into the wall and Maya sighed with relief, ignoring the pain of the impact as the wall crumbled.

The girls didn't bother to look back. They just ran for their lives.

Screams and shouts echoed across the village as Luis's men searched for the girls, turning the village upside down. Right now, there was nothing they could do but wait it out.

"We have to get out of here," Maya rasped in Joss's ear as they ran to the trees. The night was lit up by a quarter moon, and

Maya was both grateful and annoyed. It lit their way of escape, but would show their pursuers exactly where the girls were.

"We can make it to the road. Head to the nearest village."

Maya nodded gasping for air. "That should give Nik enough time to find us. Let's go."

She held onto Joss's arm as they crashed into the brush. Denser trees bordered the land, providing much needed cover for the two escaping girls.

But, it was hard to remain silent as they moved through the brush. The overhanging branches of palms and other wide-leaved trees crashed around them, the sound deafening to Maya's ears.

As they ran through the trees, Maya and Joss shared a terrified glance as shouts rose from the village. Glancing back at the valley, they made out a trail of bobbing torches.

They'd been seen.

The two girls ran faster, too late to care if their movements made a noise. The howls of dogs barking in the distance filled Maya with fear.

"Dogs?" squeaked Joss as they ran.

"Crap. I don't want to fry any dogs to save our lives."

She'd already killed a man.

"Let's hope it doesn't come to that," Joss managed to say as they raced out of the trees and came to a barreling stop in front of a narrow dirt road.

As she ran, Maya couldn't get the image of Claudia out of her mind. Was she so upset she'd conjured up her aunt's face inside of Rosa's memory? Maya shoved the thoughts from her mind and cursed Nik for not coming to their aid. Sure they'd escaped and could probably get to safety but the big question was where the hell was Nik and what was keeping him.

And, when would he come to get them out of here?

"Which way?" asked Joss, staring up and down the dark road. Maya stiffened. What a mess they were in. Joss's life was in danger now thanks to Maya. What if something happened to Joss?

But now was not the time to be faltering, allowing a head filled with negative thoughts to distract her. She could do that well enough after they were safely home.

"Check your GPS," Maya urged as she studied the trees behind them, keeping an eye out.

Seconds later Joss whooped softly. "That village Pedro spoke of is nearby. Merida."

"Let's move." Maya grabbed Joss's hand and they ran. They had to hoof it, and still keep an ear out for the gang. "Shit. I think following the road will be dangerous."

"No choice. Just run faster."

Maya snorted, but ran faster.

CHAPTER 28

THANKFULLY THE ROAD didn't run in a straight line. Instead, it curved back and forth, snaking just enough to keep the girls out of sight of the men in pursuit. Ten minutes later they reached the outskirts of a moderately-sized town and Maya could hear music.

"What's going on?" she mumbled to herself as they hunkered down behind a broken mud brick wall.

"Looks like Dia de los Muertos." Joss rasped. "That's Day of the Dead-"

"I know what that means," snapped Maya. "It's the perfect cover."

Joss nodded, not bothered with Maya's tone. "For you, maybe. Any gringa in this town is now at risk because of me."

"Well, you don't have to be gringa, do you?" Maya rummaged inside her backpack and handed Joss her compact. As they made a mad dash for the nearest narrow street. "That's a good deal darker than your skin tone. Cover your face, neck and hands with that. As soon as we get into the village, we can find another disguise."

Joss nodded, and dabbed as she ran. Maya marveled at her

skill. Minutes later she was all done. "Give me one of those tees you brought," Joss said.

They skidded to a stop at the border of the town and Maya gave Joss a blood-red tee, chosen because blood-stains tended to be less visible on red. Joss promptly fashioned a headscarf out of it, tucking the sleeves neatly into the back.

She managed to pass for not-so-white.

"You need darker eyes."

"No time," Joss whispered pulling Maya behind the house. She pointed behind them as two men cleared the road and began to hurry toward the village.

Without a word, Maya turned and ran deeper into the city. The girls didn't stop until they hit the main street and had to skid to a halt in order to avoid barreling straight into a float carrying a mariachi band and two dancing senoritas.

Maya heaved a sigh of relief and pulled Joss into the crowd. "We need to find a place that sells masks and costumes."

"Perfect." Joss grumbled. "This is like the part in the movies where everything that can go wrong does."

Maya refused to justify that with a response.

They scurried back and forth through the crowd until they spotted a handful of carts selling masks- black and white, and mostly skulls, wigs, and random clothing. Good thing her dad had thought to include the Pesos, although it wasn't as if they were spending hundreds of dollar's worth.

A few minutes later, Joss wore a black waist-length wig, a mask that was half skeleton and half porcelain doll, and a skirt that came to her ankles.

Maya was dressed similarly, only she also wore a white peasant blouse in place of her blue running jacket. They were indistinguishable from the rest of the revelers now, and the girls slowed their movements to a leisurely walk, keeping pace with the procession.

The music was deafening, which put Maya on edge. They

wouldn't be able to hear the men if they caught up with them. But still, so far, they were safe.

The better question was where in Patala was Nik?

Maya's heart twisted with fear. What could be keeping him?

Maya sighed. She had no choice but to hope Nik would come as soon as he was able to. Which wasn't soon enough as far as she was concerned.

The crowd weaved along the streets of the town, and it seemed they were getting louder as they moved. Maya sensed that at the end of this street would prove to be the finale of the event.

The faces around her were painted in varying shapes and sizes of skulls, people wore the strangest of clothing.

On the Day of the Dead the living honored the dead. People remembered those in their families that have passed as well as ancestors long gone. The celebration was considerably fashionable in the Western world, which was why it was already familiar to Maya.

Sure there were lots of tourists lurking around, and it was easy enough to identify them. None resembled Maya or Joss, which was an incredible relief. Maya didn't want to endanger any more innocent lives just because she and Joss were running for their own.

She glanced over her shoulder, and her gut twisted. The first of the men were near enough to the girls that all they had to do was turn their heads to find them.

With the masks covering their faces, Maya and Joss were fairly safe.

One of the men walked by so close he could have grabbed her hair and dragged her out of the procession if he wanted to.

For once her darker skin was coming in handy.

Joss was another story altogether. Despite the darker foundation hiding her skin, her paleness was visible every time she moved her arms, every time the sleeve of her shirt rose higher.

Maya lifted a hand and placed it on Joss's arm, pressing it down to her side. Joss gave her a questioning glance, but didn't resist.

As Maya turned, she caught sight of another thug standing on the other side of the road. He was staring at Joss, looking straight at her neck. Where the line of dark foundation met her pale skin.

As he yelled for backup, Maya grabbed Joss's hand and pulled. "They made us."

"Shit." Joss swore a little more until she was satisfied.

"Stay low," said Maya, pulling Joss down below shoulder level of the people around them. They drew curious looks, but other than that few people paid them any attention. "Come, we should head in the opposite direction. They'll expect us to go forward."

Joss nodded, peering between legs and arms. "You're right. They're scanning the crowd ahead and hurrying down towards the front of the procession."

The girls headed back in the direction from which they'd come, keeping low and weaving between the people.

Though a smart idea, as they reached the float carrying the mariachi band, Maya looked up to find they were surrounded. Where the men had come from, she had no idea. Perhaps they were better at this whole cloak-and-dagger chasing-the-innocent-victim routine than she'd predicted.

Though Maya was certainly no innocent victim.

She glared at them in disgust. Then pulling Joss to her, she turned and ran. They were probably going straight into the arms of the rest of the men, but they had to keep going. They had to hope Nick could save them.

A gunshot rang out across the crowd, and everyone fell to the ground, the action so uniform it seemed practiced.

Maya hated the thought that these people were so used to these thugs that they knew exactly what to do when they turned up and blasted a gun over their head.

A familiar voice whispered in Maya's ear. "I'm here. What the hell did you two get yourselves into?"

Maya shifted her gaze to Nik and glared at him, fury making her head hot. But she didn't have time to take her anger out on him.

Woman screamed and men hushed them into silence. The crowd submitted, afraid.

Gunmen yelled something into a crowd and Joss leaned closer to Maya, unable to see Nik as he still had his glamor surrounding him. "He's telling them to give us up or he'll start killing children."

"Shit. Just great." Maya said. She looked up at Nik. "We're going to have to create a miraculous event here."

"What do you mean?" asked Joss. "We can't just disappear from the middle of this crowd."

Maya gritted her teeth. "Yeah, he'd only start killing people. He needs to see it with his own eyes."

Maya's stomach tightened as they made their way through the crowd and slipped out of the procession with Nik close to Maya's side. One of the men near Maya held tightly onto the leash of a German Shepherd, it's yellow teeth bared, saliva spraying as he barked at the girls.

"Hey, you," yelled Maya, getting the man's attention.

He was about twenty feet ahead and spun at the sound of her voice. People in the crowd remained silent, watching in fear. The creep grinned, then looked behind Maya at the band. He waved an imperious hand. Seemed like he was enjoying his newly acquired power.

On his instruction, the band began playing again. And the procession continued, the people moving along, casting curious glances their way. Yet no one stopped to help them. Maya understood.

Nevertheless, she had little choice. "Right, let's do this."

The men hurried closer, waving a hand at his cohorts behind. They closed in on the girls, providing efficient cover from the crowd. Maya had no doubt their lives were in jeopardy. The gang would have to make an example of the girls to the village.

He'd either kill the two of them here, then haul the bodies back to the village, or take them back alive and execute them in front of the villagers.

Maya wasn't about to let that happen.

She held tightly onto Joss's hand. "Here goes."

She looked up at Nik. "You're on."

Nik gave a sharp nod.

When Maya heard the shouts of confusion and frustration rise around her, she knew Nik's glamor had done its job.

She grabbed Joss's hand and pulled her to the side of the street, and they tiptoed down a small alley. They'd managed to crouch in the shadows when Nik threw off his glamor and appeared beside them.

Maya glared at him. "What took you so long?"

He gave them an apologetic glance, and held out his hands. The girls grabbed onto his hands, but neither one was smiling.

CHAPTER 29

NIK TRANSPORTED THEM away, depositing them in the front hall of Maya's home.

"I'm really sorry. I came as soon as I got the message."

Joss shoved Maya aside and got right up close to Nik's face. "If you aren't going to be backup, don't say you will. You've no idea what almost happened."

Despite being equally pissed off, Maya lifted her eyebrows and tried not to laugh at the sight of Joss, a mere human, getting bossy with a demigod with enough powers to incinerate her with the flick of his finger.

But Nik didn't seem offended in the least. He frowned and looked at Maya.

"I can only guess it must have something to do with sketchy cell reception in the area."

"The GPS worked," snapped Maya.

"But only when we were on the road," said Joss.

Maya had to force herself to take a slow breath as she digested the reality of sketchy cellphone coverage.

Still, Nik looked apologetic. "Tell me what happened?"

She shrugged, gritting her teeth. "It was nothing. We're fine."

Something soft and furry brushed her hand and she reached out and rubbed Sabala's head. She'd needed him and he hadn't been able to be with her. Something else that had gone wrong.

Joss rounded on her. "Fine? You call this fine? You were almost killed. Let's not forget the part where you were almost raped because you thought it was a fantastic idea to push me aside and take my place. You seem to be making this a habit."

Nik took a step towards Maya. "Maya?" His voice was questioning, but it held an edge to it.

He was angry at *her*?

She glared at him.

"Yes," she said, keeping a voice even. She really didn't want to lose it with him. "We did get into a bit of danger. But I had it under control. I used my fire and killed him before he could do anything to hurt us."

Maya's voice broke as she spoke the words. She stepped backwards until she reached the staircase, and sank heavily onto the bottom step, while the hellhound whined and curled up on the step beside her.

"Maya?" asked Joss. She sat down on the other side of Maya. "What's the matter?"

"Apart from coming so close to being very dead, I just killed a man." She fisted fingers that had begun to shake.

But, when Joss rubbed her back, the action gave her a little bit of comfort.

"You can't blame yourself for what happened. You did the only thing you could to protect us. And he wasn't exactly the nicest man on the planet."

Maya looked at her. "It doesn't matter whether he was nice or not. He was a human being." Maya got to her feet and began to pace. She wasn't sure what to do with her hands. At first she put them on her hips, and then she threw them up in the air. "I just killed a *man* for God's sake."

Nik took a step closer to her, taking hold of her arms and

bringing her to a standstill. "And what does that mean to you Maya?"

Maya stood up at his face. "What do *you* mean?" she snapped at him.

Nik watched her face. "You're upset because you killed a man. But why are you really upset. What about this death is bothering you so much?"

Maya let out a deep sigh. "I don't know. It's just . . . I need some space." She pulled her elbow out of Nik's grasp and ran upstairs, ignoring Sabala who kept close behind her.

Inside her room, she shut the door, coming so close to slamming it but catching herself in time. She wasn't angry with anyone in particular. To be totally honest, it was herself she couldn't understand.

She'd lied to Nik when he asked what she meant. She knew exactly what was upsetting her.

She'd killed a man.

He was evil and he'd probably intended to kill her, and much, much worse. No doubt he was guilty of doing such horrible things to numerous other people before her. So he'd deserved it.

What made Maya furious was she believed he deserved it. Which meant the demons were no longer the only bad guys in her book. Up until now, her anger and rage had been focused solely on the demons, the Rakshasas.

When her parents had mentioned mercenaries, snipers and bombers hired by the KALIMA to take out demons, Maya had just shrugged: that was part of life. Killing demons. But now she had to accept demons were not the only bad guys.

In fact, humans could be just as bad, if not worse.

Whether demon or human, she'd have to eliminate the threat without hesitation.

But what did that make her?

Maya shuddered as she moved towards her bed. With a sigh, she sat at the foot of her bed. She was still wearing the same blouse and skirt they'd used to hide themselves on the street. The mask hung from her fingertips, and she turned it over and studied the face. Half skull and half porcelain face. The thing was almost pretty.

She held her fingers up to her gaze, aware now of the soot stain from touching Luis's burning chest.

She shivered and threw her arms around her waist.

She was slowly becoming a different person, one she wasn't sure she liked.

Sure, she had Kali's powers, one's that made her almost invincible. But that didn't give her the right to use it to kill. Even if it was to kill bad guys.

She sighed, rubbing her forehead, uncaring that she was smudging black soot all over her skin. As much as she tried to evade the reality, the truth was she would do it. Whether the bad guy was demon or human, she had to accept that when faced with that choice, she'd kill them. Just like she'd killed Luis.

She stared at her open palms again, watching as her fire slowly surfaced and glowed. She had living flame within her. She was a walking time-bomb. Able to annihilate people, towns and possibly even cities. The more she used the power, the more powerful she got.

The more dangerous she became.

She was beginning to understand why Claudia saw her as a threat. Maybe it had something to do with Maya causing Claudia's injuries, but it was more likely what Maya represented. She was a conduit to a goddess. Maybe it was time she spoke directly to Kali about the way she felt.

Maya sighed.

When she got to her feet, the load that had weighed on her shoulders, had weighed her soul down, felt a little lighter.

And suddenly she understood what faith was all about. It was about sharing the burden of life with someone much more powerful than you. Maybe not in person, but in a spiritual sense.

It was about accepting the harshness of living, and blending it with the joy of knowing this existence is only a small part of the universe of life.

Maya smiled as she headed into the shower. She had a job to do. And she no longer had any qualms about doing it.

CHAPTER 30

WHEN MAYA FINALLY made it to her dad's study with Sabala in tow, she couldn't have been more surprised at the utter chaos she faced. A very effective tornado had run through the small room, strategically sticking to specific storage locations.

Smart tornado.

"What happened?" she asked, aghast, pausing on the threshold.

Said smart tornado had flung books off the floor-to-ceiling bookshelves, emptied drawers onto the carpet, and had figured it was good karma to throw every single piece of paper onto the floor.

Her dad was standing beside the window, drapes drawn, which was quite strange because he loved having light - either sun or moon didn't matter - shining into the room. He was studying the mess, a strange look in his eye. Leela was focused on rifling through papers and drawers, looking for something.

Her parents both glanced up when she entered.

Dev took a deep breath. "It happened exactly as I expected."

"What happened?" Maya repeated, feeling her stress levels rise.

"Your mom and I both knew KALIMA would send someone to find out what we know. And the best way to do that is to see all our paperwork."

Maya stared at her dad's desk. Something was missing. "And a certain laptop?" she asked.

"Yes," he said. But he didn't look too concerned.

Maya's eyes narrowed as she studied him. "You were expecting this? What did you do?"

He shrugged. "I transferred all my data *and* I deleted the hard-drive. There's a bit of code written in there too, so soon as someone tries to hack into the computer, they will upload a virus into their entire network."

Maya laughed.

Leela got to her feet and dusted off her knees. "It got a little bit rushed while you were gone."

"You guys were here when it happened?

"Yes, good thing we had the panic rooms installed."

Maya raised her eyebrows. She'd always thought her parents were being a little dramatic when they'd installed the safe rooms two years ago. But now she saw the wisdom in it.

"Were you guys hurt?"

They both shook their heads. "No," said her dad. "We were upstairs. I'd expected them to come at night, thinking we wouldn't hear them. Fortunately, they aren't as smart as they think they are."

Maya would be banking on the latter.

"We hid as soon as we heard the noise. Thank goodness your dad insisted on a second panic room upstairs."

Maya smiled and threaded her way inside the room. She wanted to help but wasn't sure where to start. "So what now?" Sabala remained on the threshold as if he knew he would be of no help.

"Now we get our stuff and get out. Your bags are already

packed. We were only waiting for you guys to return. Hopefully Nik can transport the lot of us out of here."

Maya nodded, feeling something twist in her stomach. "Do I have time to check my room?"

Dev shook his head. "If Nick is here we need to leave now."

"I think Joss is in her room. I'll have a look around for the demigod. He was here when we got home twenty minutes ago."

"You should have come straight to me Maya. Had I known you were here for so long, I would have insisted we leave immediately."

"Sorry, Dad," she said. "I have a few things I'm dealing with right now, and I just needed some time to myself. If I knew how urgent it was I would have come to you the moment we arrived." She glanced at the dark drapes, hiding them from watchful eyes. "You think they'll come back so soon?"

Dev nodded. "Yes. They didn't get what they wanted. They'll be watching the place, and if you went near any windows they'd know you're here."

Maya raised an eyebrow. "What if they have thermal imaging?"

"If they do, then we're in deep shit," said her mom.

Maya raised her eyebrows and would have reprimanded her mom's language but Leela continued, "Everything is ready to go. You get Joss and we'll meet you in the kitchen. And take the dog with you."

Leela was all businesslike but Maya could sense the drama was taking a toll on her. She'd already lost her best friend, and now she was about to lose her house. A place that had been a home to her for the last fifteen years.

Maya turned on her heel and hurried upstairs. Sabala trotted at her side as she headed straight to Joss who was busy packing her backpack, looking a little confused. She looked up at Maya. "Have you seen my jeans?"

"Just grab what you need. Mom already packed everything

else. If you're looking for something it's probably downstairs in a suitcase waiting for you."

Joss's eyes widened. "What's going on?"

She was already throwing her rucksack over her shoulder and hurrying to the door.

Maya filled her in as the three headed downstairs.

"Good thing we won't miss school," was all Joss said.

When they entered the kitchen Maya was relieved to see her mum had found Nik. The five of them gathered around the kitchen table, tension simmering between them.

"Right, we'd better get-"

The window shattered, Sabala yelped and a teargas canister landed in the middle of the kitchen, narrowly missing the wooden table.

Nik grabbed Joss and Maya. "I'll be back. Sabala will stay with you. Keep down and hold your breath," he said to Maya's parents before jumping the girls to Patala, leaving them in the room Maya had used on their last visit.

He left without a word to fetch her parents.

Maya stood frozen in place, her mind going over and over the craziness of the last few seconds, even the beauty of the room with its fountains, and wide balconies did nothing.

Her heart hammered just at the thought that this could all be Claudia's doing.

The shattering of glass echoed in her ears. The clatter of the canister as it hit the terracotta tile. Her mom's gasp as she caught sight of the cylinder rolling along the floor.

Maya's life was slowly coming apart at the seams.

And as Maya stood there, frozen in shock and frustration, all she could think about was the burn mark in the middle of the wooden table in their kitchen.

The burn mark she'd made the day Nik had told her who he really was.

And strangely enough, the thought she'd never see that mark

again, or the table itself, made her want to fall to her knees and burst into tears. But she had to be strong. Joss stood beside her, hugging herself tightly.

Maya curled her pinky around Joss's little finger, and the two girls stood there, waiting for Nik to bring Maya's parents.

She only let out her breath when they all appeared what felt like long moments later. Both girls rushed to Maya's parents as soon as they materialized. Maya didn't resist when her mum took her into her arms and held tight. Even the hellhound stood to the side to give them space.

For now, neither of the girls were bad-ass demon killers.

They were just kids without a home.

CHAPTER 31

MAYA'S FAMILY SPENT only enough time in Patala for a good night's sleep and breakfast of sweet chai tea and delicious soji halwa pudding.

The decision was made to split the family into two groups with Leela and Joss heading to Rarotonga a few hours later to investigate another dancer's death. With the time difference they had a few hours to play with before sunrise in the pacific island.

They would be accompanied by Sabala, to investigate another dancer's death, and Maya and her dad were going to a safe house on the outskirts of Mumbai because so many of the victims originated within the Indian subcontinent.

Lord Yama was of the opinion that the sorcerer was located in the Mumbai area. Maya had had the very same suspicion when Nik had given her the list of the most recent deaths.

Maya had kept two things to herself so as not to worry her parents any more. The seductive pull of the dancer's energy on Maya, and the vision of Claudia in Rosa's memories. No sense in worrying them about something that could just be Maya's imagination.

Father and daughter arrived with their luggage into a muggy

Mumbai evening. Nik had delivered them inside a large airy hall that looked like it belonged in Victorian England.

Not your typical Indian home.

Beyond the air of desertion, Maya could see how grand it had once been. The house would have belonged to the British during their early occupation of the country, which explained the state of disrepair. In some parts of India, the hatred for the British was still strong.

Seconds later, as if their arrival had tripped an alarm, the tapping of two sets of boots echoed along the hall to their left. Two men arrived, and it took one sniff to identify them: Rakshasas.

Maya's instinct told her to attack, but she knew well enough that Nik's personal guard contained more demons than humans. She studied each of their faces, making a note of their unique scent.

Once she knew their individual essence, she'd be able to tell just with her nose, exactly where they were within the house.

Sometimes Maya really liked her nose.

The guards stopped just inside the door and bowed to their Lord. Nik waited until they'd straightened then beckoned them closer.

"Please show Maya and her family to their rooms."

"Yes, My Lord. The Jungle Wing has been prepared for your guests as per your request."

Jungle Wing?

Though curious, Maya remained silent as the guards led them inside, showing them to rooms up on the second floor, toward the rear of the house.

They walked along cracked marble tiled floors, and stared at wall hangings and tapestries that showed frolicking maidens, cows and cowherds in expansive fields.

Once they'd left their bags in their rooms, both with expansive views of the jungle, obviously, they returned to meet with Nick.

He was holding a file, studying the contents. As they drew closer he reached for a small travel bag and handed it to Dev.

Inside were passports and paperwork and ID cards verifying their roles with Interpol.

Then he dropped the file he'd been reading onto the table beside a thick stack of brown folders. "These are the documents from dead dancer cases that have been reported over the last two months. It would be a good idea to discreetly investigate them while you're on the ground. The guards will arrange transport for you, as and when you require it. They will also provide weapons should you need them."

"What is this place?" asked Maya studying the airy ceiling as her dad scanned the files.

"A base we use when we send people to this part of the world, not that we have anything near the size of KALIMA. I use this house every so often, and we have two guards here permanently. We keep the outside looking as unkempt as possible to deter nosy neighbors."

Maya gave the guard standing beside the door a discreet glance.

Nik nodded. "Yes, they are both Rakshasa. I knew that wouldn't get past your nose." He gave a smile and Maya was well aware he was trying for a little bit of levity to ease the tension in the room.

She was still a little angry with him even though it had not been his fault. Things had been so hectic during the last few hours in Patala they hadn't had time to talk. Maya supposed more time would pass before they managed it.

For now, she smiled even though she didn't feel like it. Her dad though, was busy combing through the files.

Maya took Nik aside. "You don't have to worry about us. Just leave the papers and we'll have everything sorted. If you can, let us know if there are any new cases to investigate. We'll get to those as soon as possible. I prefer to see a fresh case rather than one that happened a month ago."

Nik cocked his chin at the report. "I hate to say it but we do have a recent one. It's just outside Mumbai city." He glanced at his phone, clearly distracted by whatever job he had to do that had nothing to do with Maya or dead dancers.

Maya smiled. She wished she could tell him not to go, but she understood Nik had a job to do. She was not the clingy girlfriend.

"I'll be fine. Now stop worrying and go do what you have to do." She made a shooing motion with her hands.

"I wish I could stay and help. But there are other reports needing attention."

Maya lifted a hand, imperiously waving his excuses away. "Stop explaining. You have a job to do, and responsibilities. You don't need to be looking after me."

Nik didn't smile. "Look what happened the last time I said I'd look after you."

"Yeah. There is that." Maya said, her tone emotionless. Then she gave his chest a small punch. "Whatever you do, don't go blaming yourself for that."

"Sure. I'm definitely not responsible for your near death experience." Maya could hear the self-deprecation in his voice. "I promised I'd be there to take you to safety. But I put you in such danger." He stopped talking and ran fingers along his temples.

She leaned forward and hugged him. "You'd better get going. We don't need you hanging around here wasting our time." She wiggled her fingers at him while giving him a small smile. He shook his head and smiled back before disappearing in a flurry of bronze and copper smoke.

Maya turned and strode to the table and studied the folders. "Which is the most recent?" she asked her dad.

He handed her the folder. "Last night."

Maya felt her stomach tighten, nerves like giant spears stabbing her into readiness. "This is exactly what we need." Her eyes widened as her words sank in. "Shit. I didn't mean that. What I meant to say was that the best way I can help is by studying a *recent* crime. The new scene may tell me more than the dream did."

"Then we'd better get going," said Dev as he turned and waved the guard forward.

Maya controlled the urge to wrinkle her nose at the Eu de Demon as the Rakshasa drew closer. The familiar scent of rotting meat and spices made her want to hurl.

The demon seemed oblivious to Maya's problem, and stood beside Dev, listening intently as he was given instructions to bring round a vehicle.

Maya opened the folder and studied the report.

Agrasen Ki Baoli. An ancient well on the outskirts of Mumbai had been the location of another body. From what Maya read the police had only just left the scene. She was disappointed she wouldn't encounter the body of the girl, but she had to admit, even if it was only to herself, that she was a little bit glad. She was still afraid. What if that strange energy threatened to take control of her again as it had in the theatre in London.

It didn't take long before the car was ready, and Maya and her dad climbed in. Their demon chauffeur drove away from the large house, toward a ten-foot-high fence. Even the iron gate guarding the main entrance was monstrous.

Exiting the grounds of the estate, they headed south towards the city. The Mother's Temple was somewhere out there and Maya felt a deep desire to visit. She figured she'd get the opportunity before they left India, but didn't forget the place had a strong link to KALIMA.

Another part of her life she may have to sacrifice because of Claudia and the agency.

The driver headed across the city keeping to the outer road.

As they drew closer to their destination he glanced over his shoulder and met her father's eyes.

"Do you know anything about this place you're going to?" he asked. The look he gave Dev implied he didn't have much confidence in Maya's dad.

Dev Rao wasn't exactly Vin Diesel. He was a quiet, unassuming man, small in stature. But for his size, he possessed a power within him that could rival the strongest men.

He cleared his throat and said, "From what I remember, the well is said to have been haunted almost a hundred years ago."

The demon nodded as he took a turn into a narrow side road. "One hundred and eighteen years ago, three teenaged girls killed themselves in the well."

Dev nodded. "I believe the well has dried up?"

"Yes. The water disappeared about two decades ago, although that didn't stop the tales of the place being haunted. It did, of course, stop the drownings."

Maya wondered why the body would have been found in this particular location. A well, of all things.

Only when the demon brought the car to a stop on the dusty road that overlooked the well, did Maya understand why a dancer might come here.

She also understood why she shouldn't have come at all.

CHAPTER 32

I T WAS TWILIGHT, and the shadows grew longer, making everything seem much more ominous. The well though technically a hole in the ground, was all bricked up nice and symmetrically designed, and looked as far from a well as was possible.

No, this well was something ancient. Hundreds of steps descended down into the rectangular entrance of Agrasen Ki Baoli. Along the three outer walls, dozens of alcoves and stone shelves looked out like empty eyes.

At one time they would have contained statues of gods and goddesses and dancing maidens, but those had been gone a long time. Now, dark shadows played along the walls, bringing into stark contrast the cracked and broken brickwork.

Not a place that welcomed you with open arms.

Goosebumps covered Maya's skin as her body picked up the strange energy of the place. An energy that was horribly familiar to Maya. She almost expected to hear drums and the jingle of bells.

At the top of the stairs, Maya turned her attention to the wide landing. Its open space and smoothly laid stone floor would be easy to dance on.

And, remote.

The seclusion would have provided a place to practice in private, as the papers had confirmed the well was closed to visitors after hours.

Again, Maya glanced down into the depths of the well. A sudden image clouded her vision, water glinting in the depths of the well, the alcoves filled with deities gleaming with gold and jewels, and thousands and thousands of clay lamps, filling the walls, and lining the steps all the way to the bottom.

Maya blinked the thoughts away, unnerved by the intrusion of the sudden vision and by its strength. She shivered and shook the feeling off as she got closer to the platform.

The chalk lines that had outlined the corpse of the girl, gleamed in the moonlight. The police had also cordoned off the scene of the crime; large concrete poles that squared off the scene, yellow fluorescent tape kept people off the evidence.

Although the scene was macabre, Maya's attention was repeatedly drawn into the depths of the well. She abandoned all attempts to concentrate on the scene and walked to the edge of the stairs, staring into the very center, searching for what had triggered her instinctive curiosity.

Darkness flooded the depths and Maya couldn't be sure how far the steps went. From what she remembered hearing, these ancient wells were constructed to access the water which had been a precious commodity. It wasn't unheard of for the constructors to dig hundreds of meters into the ground.

Near the bottom a waterline marked the walls, delineating where the water had last risen to. Greyed and dusty, it was clearly old and confirmed the demon's information.

Below the waterline, the walls were smooth and remained without decoration. Above the line they were beautiful. Some alcoves were much deeper, almost acting as a balcony.